Andrew Lee

# The
# Intimate Sensations
### of Andrew Lee

Anonymous

Chief Researcher : Andrew Lee

HEADLINE

Printed and bound in Great Britain by
Collins Manufacturing, Glasgow

HEADLINE BOOK PUBLISHING PLC
Headline House
79 Great Titchfield Street
London W1P 7FN

# Part I

## CHAPTER 1

Marcy dropped her eyes to the polished wooden floor as she stood before Mr. Van Couvering. She shifted her feet uneasily and again wondered what she, an 18-year-old from High Flats, was doing here.

How in the world did she ever think she'd be able to take care of his and Mrs. Van Couvering's young daughter adequately? Yes, it was true that she'd been hired to take care of the little girl only when Mrs. Van Couvering was out shopping or doing charity work or spending time at a spa. And yes, it was true that she'd often taken care of her younger sisters, but this—this was different. It was so awesome, so sophisticated.

Marcy swallowed nervously, wiping her wet palm on her black pleated skirt. The house was so large, the gardens so imposingly neat, the shrubs so perfectly symmetrical, the acres of flowers so pristinely arranged.

And Mr. Van Couvering. A powerfully deep voice, long sinewy build, thick dark brows and black hair over a rugged, handsome face and square jaw.

Mrs. Van Couvering seemed to fade into the background, a small, dark-haired woman in proper dark suits and silk blouses. But Mr. Van Couvering, he was quite something else. Even in the few hours she'd been here, Marcy could tell he was the presence, that the house, the servants and the family revolved around his wishes.

Breathing deeply, she resolved to do her very best. The employment agency would not have sent her if it were not confident of her abilities.

"Please, Marcy, do look up." Mr. Van Couvering spoke gently, his deep voice breaking into her thoughts. "I understand that this can be frightening the first time. But, honestly, our daughter, Alexandra, is kind and well-behaved, and you won't find yourself overwhelmed by her at all."

Marcy smiled gratefully and flipped her lustrous blonde hair over her shoulders. Her dark blue eyes, framed by their blonde lashes, widened appreciatively. And instantly, she knew she would like him, that he would ease her transition.

"As the employment agency personnel probably told you," Mr. Van Couvering continued, leaning against his massive mahogany desk, "we frequently go abroad on business. So," he smiled widely, "I

2

do hope you won't mind going to London or Paris."

Marcy giggled in relief. "No, sir, not at all."

"Come, look out at the view." He beckoned, his hand outstretched.

Marcy walked over to the desk and peered out the window. She spied a wrought-iron fence, shielding the 75-foot swimming pool from prying eyes of strangers and erring feet of small children. In the distance, she heard the steady rhythm of a tennis ball lobbing against rackets. And suddenly, she smiled fully, hugging her arms to enfold her well-shaped, generous breasts. Yes, indeed, she thought she'd like this.

"What do you think?" Mr. Van Couvering looked down at her, his breath glancing off her ear. Unexpectedly, Marcy felt a strange feeling lurch through her. It was a feeling she'd had only once before. With Kurt.

"I, I—" she stammered, unprepared for the tingling. She heaved a sigh, awaiting the departure of that unfamiliar feeling. "It's beautiful. And I promise," Marcy turned toward him and raised her large eyes to look at her employer, "I promise to do such a wonderful job taking care of Alexandra that you won't ever have cause to worry."

"I have every confidence." Mr. Van Couvering circled his arm around her shoulders for an instant, and winked. "Mrs. Van Couvering has prepared a synopsis of your responsibilities and your privileges. Now, Alexandra's probably up from her nap, so why don't I introduce you two?"

So saying, he stood, and with a light hand on her elbow, ushered Marcy from the library into the immense front hall with its marble floors and up the five-foot wide winding staircase to his daughter's nursery.

Marcy scarcely dared to breathe. It was so different, so bewildering, so exciting, here in the middle of Delaware's horse country, country clubs and mansions. She, little Marcy, just out of high school, just a day away from her first real experience. Or almost. She blushed to think of it.

It was only supposed to be a regular night of kissing, of course, the kind they'd had together for the past year. She would open her mouth to receive his tongue, but never anything else. She'd often felt his hands begin to roam from her back or shoulders, but she'd always sent them back, confidently knowing that he would obey. She knew, in fact, they both knew, that he didn't really mean to wander, that they both intended to remain chaste until their marriage. And they'd be married after her year as an *au pair*.

But somehow, last night, it was different.

Marcy knew she was leaving the midwest for awhile, that she needed to see more before she settled down with Kurt and the five kids they both wanted, the kind of family they'd both grown up in. So she was kissing him goodbye for awhile, a final kiss that would set her on the road a little better, and thank him for having honored her in

4

the past. It would be one last big kiss.

So last night, they had walked around the pond where they usually walked and listened to the bull frogs mating. Abruptly, she sat down on the grass, leaning against the large boulder. Kurt sat next to her, his strong, bull-like body smelling of the outdoors, so different from Mr. Van Couvering's tall, graceful one that smelled of fine cologne.

Kurt leaned toward her, wrapping his arms around her back, as always. He felt for her lips. Gently, he ran his tongue over her bottom lip, then her top lip. Enticed, she opened them slightly. As never before, a sort of heat invaded her. She shifted, trying to smother the tingling that was creeping through her body.

She pressed her mouth against his and felt his tongue probe hers. In a second, one of his hands lay on her breast. Then she felt his other hand also, as ten fingers kneaded her flesh that had never been touched that way before. Her heart pumping, she pressed her breasts against his fingers and moved again so that, unknowingly, her knee wedged beneath his body.

Kurt toyed with her nipples through her summer blouse and she pressed toward him, urging him onward. Gently, he laid her back on the grassy hilltop, and amid the bull frogs' mating calls, he lay on top of her and rubbed against her.

She gasped in shock as she felt, for the first time, his manhood against her very private regions. Instinctively, she tried to wiggle away, but he would not have it.

Kurt squirmed against her and played with her taut nipples. And while she knew she should stop, that this was wrong, that they had promised never to do even this much, she couldn't stop. She strained against him, hoping he would pull up her blouse and place his fingers directly on her breasts.

Then, suddenly, his entire body stiffened, his tongue thrust so deeply that she thought she would suffocate. And then he stopped and lay, panting, against her.

"What happened?" She asked, mystified that he had stopped so abruptly.

"It's over." He rolled off her.

"Oh, no, not yet," she wailed softly. It couldn't be. It had just started. She had just felt that incredible heat spreading through her. "Oh, please, Kurt." Hungrily, she reached for his hand, now laying lightly on her slim hip, and drew it under her blouse. But he didn't respond.

How could you do this to me, she wanted to yell, but she knew she couldn't. It would be an inappropriate reaction; girls shouldn't want these sorts of things. Besides, she was probably wrong to have gone this far. Tears choked her, though she didn't know why. Again she pressed his hand onto her breast.

"Marce, I'm sorry. Look." He pointed toward his crotch.

She looked at the spreading wet spot festooned onto the front of his jeans.

"Oh, dear," she sighed. She'd never seen that before, but she knew what it was. And she knew that he'd want no more from her.

Sadly, she pushed herself away, trying to block out that invasive heat.

"Forgive me? It won't happen again."

She nodded dully. "It would have been wonderful. The kissing and hugging and stuff." She dared not say more.

"Next time. When you get back from the east. We'll do it for real. Ok?" Kurt touched her lips with his fingers.

"I'll wait," she replied, kissing his palm.

Now she smiled at little Alexandra. Prettily, the child curtsied to Marcy and held out her hand. "I am very glad to meet you."

Marcy knelt down and put out her own hand. "And I'm very glad to meet you." She glanced around the girl's room. Never had she seen so many stuffed animals, electrical gadgets, blocks and fancy dolls. "You have great toys, Alexandra. What's your favorite?"

Immediately, the girl stood and ran to a plastic farm house. "This," she pointed proudly. "Would you play with me?" She opened the little barn doors and cows and pigs and plastic farmers tumbled out.

Grinning, Marcy hiked up her skirt so she could join her new charge. She noted Mr. Van Couvering eye her thighs, well uncovered in her current position.

"Well, ladies, perhaps I'll let you two get to know each other now." Mr. Van Couvering stooped to kiss his daughter and pat Marcy familiarly on the head. "Marcy, if you want anything or have questions that the housekeeper or Mrs. Van Couvering can't answer, please see me."

"Thank you, sir." Marcy smiled frankly and followed him with her eyes as he left the room. Then she turned her attention to Alexandra.

As the afternoon waned, she found herself wondering how she'd entertain herself after Alexandra went to bed. Would she find any friends of her own age? Was there a local movie theatre or soda fountain? Where would she shop? Of course, traveling sounded glamorous and rewarding, but once she got used to it, what then? Where would she find people to bowl or sew with? Who would take her to the church dances? Well, she shrugged, she'd just have to wait and see. She was only committed for a year, and anyone could bear a year without too much loneliness.

She and Alexandra dined together nightly in the tiny flowered dinette off the kitchen. Theresa, the cook, prepared the meals, and the butler, Wayne, served them. Marcy was amazed that all she truly had to do was keep Alexandra occupied and accompany her to lessons and friends' houses. Lawrence, the chauffeur, would drive them.

Happily, the days drifted into one another. Marcy scarcely saw Mrs. Van Couvering except when she stopped by to play with Alexandra for awhile each day. She always seemed preoccupied. But she and Mr. Van Couvering got along well, bantering and laughing with one another at least once daily. She looked forward to meeting him in the mornings as he emerged from the library and the late afternoons at the pool or just walking on the grounds. Gratified, she sensed he liked the meetings too.

But while the days were full, the nights proved empty. She had only the television and her letters to her mother and Kurt. She waited anxiously for one of Alexandra's friends to return home from vacation with her parents and her French *au pair*, hoping there'd be a friend for her also. But, still, despite it all, she wasn't unhappy.

Now Alexandra tugged at her sleeve. "Marcy. Read me this book." The five-year-old held out a gaily colored book about numbers.

"Great. I love this book." Impulsively, Marcy leaned down and kissed Alexandra's curly black hair. "Come. I'll read this before bed."

They walked from the playroom where they'd been playing with the farmers into Alexandra's nursery. Marcy hoisted her into her canopied double bed, swathed in white eyelet cotton. As usual, she sat next to Alexandra as she read.

"Did Daddy and Mommy go out for dinner yet?"

"Dunno. Anyway," Marcy chucked her chin, "what's the matter with me?"

Their exchange was broken by a soft tap at the

door. It opened to Mr. Van Couvering. "Well, ladies, I just wanted to say goodnight to my little girl."

He strolled over to the bed. Marcy pulled her red pleated skirt lower on her thighs. He leaned across Marcy to kiss his child.

"Daddy, wanna sit with us?"

"Sure." Mr. Van Couvering lowered his body to the side, placing his thigh just next to Marcy's. She felt his muscles. She swallowed nervously.

And again, she felt that strange flash reel through her and come to rest between her thighs. She quivered slightly. Mr. Van Couvering placed his hand lightly on her calf. Marcy tensed.

"Perhaps I should let you two alone," he suggested.

"Nonsense," Marcy hastily said. "We always like men," she giggled.

Alexandra nodded and, within moments, was breathing in peaceful sleep.

Mr. Van Couvering stood and stretched out a hand for Marcy to pull herself up by. His hand carelessly brushed against her breast, sending a tremor through her. Frightened, she pulled away and hastily bid him goodnight as she stumbled to her room.

She closed the door and leaned against it, eyes closed, hand across her heart. Something was happening to her body. But what? And why? And why now? Ever since that night weeks ago with Kurt, the merest thought of him, and now the

10

touch of Mr. Van Couvering made her tingle.

Marcy's heart hammered throughout her body. Trying to calm herself, she eyed her room, til her glance rested on the giant canopied bed. White folds of heavy starched linen hung in great swaths from the top. Six or seven mammoth white pillows, piled on top of each other, rested against the painted white brass headboard.

She relaxed, as her breathing eased. She noticed the heavy gold cord by the edge of the bed, near her head. How fun it would be to pull it to release those swaths of fabric, enveloping the bed in a private, soft cocoon of darkness. She grinned, wondering if she'd ever be able to get it up again.

In the corner, on her bureau, was a photo of Kurt. Unexpectedly, his real face loomed before her and she thought of that night til she itched with longing. She pressed her legs together, guilty at the feelings that swelled through her. She reached in her pocket for her mother's as yet unopened letter. But, a sudden tap at the door startled her, and she left the letter in her pocket.

"Yes?" she swallowed.

"'Tis I," replied Mr. Van Couvering's deep voice.

"Yes?" Her voice quavered. What could he possibly want with her? Had she done something wrong?

"Are you all right? May I come in?"

"Of—of course." Marcy opened the door.

"I was just passing by. Mrs. Van Couvering has

gone to a meeting, so I thought I'd say goodnight to you, see if you needed anything."

Marcy swallowed, relieved not to be reprimanded, yet uncomfortable with his attention. "That's very kind of you." She looked at him and felt his eyes pierce her clothes. She smiled awkwardly, unsure of what to do.

He reached out and placed his hand gently on her shoulder. "I think you're doing a magnificent job, Marcy. You're everything my wife and I hoped you'd be. You're making Alexandra, and therefore us, very happy." He spoke softly, his lips grazing her hair.

Suddenly, despite herself, she nestled against his chest. Was it loneliness or her body's turbulence that forced her to him? Marcy felt his lips on her head as he murmured more praise. He tipped her chin up with his fingers and tipped his head down, kissing her gently on the lips.

Again, the surge. She pulled back, terrified.

"Ah, Marcy. You're afraid. Don't be." Mr. Van Couvering spoke encouragingly and drew her toward him again. "What is this but a way to show the affection we already feel for one another?"

She nodded, her heart thumping, her limbs shaking.

"Marcy," he murmured into her ear. "You would admit we're friends, wouldn't you?" He stopped and caressed her lustrous hair. "Then, believe me, I won't hurt you. I'm just showing you a way two people can become closer."

She nodded again, still trembling. But it seemed to make sense. A way for two people to become closer. She wasn't quite sure where Mr. Van Couvering was leading her, but she was sure it was further down the path than she'd ever been before. Again, that sensation between her legs threatened to spread. Hadn't she come east for experience, she asked herself. And would Kurt ever know? Would this, perhaps, make her more acceptable to him? And, after all, Marcy summed up to herself, this kissing and fondling were just ways to show affection.

With sudden decisiveness and longing, she threw her arms around his neck and lifted her lips to his. His lips forced hers apart. Ah, what harm, she said to herself. Just a kiss.

His tongue played with the corners of her mouth and ran along her teeth. He flicked it in and out of her mouth, ever so lightly.

Marcy felt his hand lift her blouse and felt long sinewy fingers unhook the clasp at her back. A warning voice blasted through her, but she did nothing to stop him. It's just my back, she thought. It's no different from Kurt. She felt him cup and lift her breasts.

With sudden urgency, he pressed against her. She felt his member rise against her belly. She gasped. Gently, he lifted her, cradled her in his arms and carried her to the bed, amidst the great pillows. Marcy saw Kurt's face in the photo smiling at her. But she closed her eyes to blot it out.

She knew she couldn't stop now. Mr. Van Couvering wouldn't let her. And the heat that suffused her body would not let her stop either.

Deftly, Mr. Van Couvering slipped off her sensible black pumps and raised her skirt. She heard the letter from her mother crinkle in the pocket. He burrowed his face into her soft neck, kissing the curve at her chin.

"Beautiful," he murmured, running his fingers langorously over her inner thighs.

Marcy strained upward to mesh her body against his, but he was sitting upright, lightly touching her thighs and, as if by accident, occasionally her crotch. She shivered at his touch. She had never before had this delicious sensation. She yearned for more, but waited, not knowing what to do, what to request.

Mr. Van Couvering slid her panties to her knees, then to her ankles, and then off onto the carpet. He reached behind her, unfastening the skirt hook and slipped the red material off her limbs onto the floor. Marcy drew her legs together and upward, as if to hide her nakedness. But now Mr. Van Couvering unbuttoned her summer blouse, and, lifting her slightly, drew it and her white cotton bra off.

She lay before him, with her voluptuous breasts over a firm stomach, and a virginal mound poised between slight hips. Gently, he plied her vulva open with his fingers. He kissed her breasts, his tongue lapping at her nipples, stiff like peach pits.

14

She heard a zipper, felt him twist to remove his clothing, then felt his lean body on hers. He pushed against her, but he would not give his manhood to her yet. His tongue teased her nipples, then ran along the curves of her breasts, her navel, as he fingered her private parts til she was wet with lust. His other hand played with the folds of her buttocks, darting in and out of her.

Then, without knowing how or when, she felt his powerful member enter her. She arched upward, straining against him. It hurt, it stretched her, but it was sumptuous. She pressed further, felt him knead her behind with one hand, press her breasts with the other, thrust his tongue deeper into her mouth. She moved her body to his rhythm, then laced her strong legs around his, urging him to enter her further.

He moved faster, taking her with him. Over and over, he plunged hard and deep. She pushed toward him, grunting and moaning. And then, the ecstacy surged through her. She clutched his back, pushed his mouth between her breasts as the luscious heat spread through her.

They lay gasping, his face buried between her flesh.

"Oh, Mr. Van Couvering," Marcy finally breathed. "Thank you, thank you so much." She smiled joyously, untangling her legs. So that's what it was all about.

"You're quite welcome," he replied, pulling back and modestly covering himself with his shirt

15

until he could slide into his pants again. He sat up, adjusting his red tie. "You're very responsive."

She nodded her thanks at the compliment.

"Who's that?" He pointed to Kurt's photo. "Your boyfriend?"

She winced, her eyes suddenly filled with regret. What had she done? Now Mr. Van Couvering wouldn't respect her anymore for cheating on her boyfriend. And neither would Kurt.

"I see," he muttered. "Have you been together?"

"No," she hesitated. "Just some kissing. But he had an orgasm once."

"Now," Mr. Van Couvering smiled comfortingly, "you've both had one. Now you are his equal. Before you weren't. Men like experienced women. Or highly responsive ones." He leaned down and patted the blonde tresses that swarmed around her face.

Marcy sat up and drew her arms across her bosom to hide herself. Ah, so there was probably no harm in doing this with Mr. Van Couvering. He seemed to be so wise. He was probably right: Kurt would admire her experience. She grinned. So it was OK after all.

"You best get some sleep. You and Alexandra probably have a big day tomorrow." Mr. Van Couvering briskly walked across the room to the door.

Marcy lay back in her bed, exhausted, completed. "So that was it," she mused. "And I liked it. I don't think I'll write about it to Kurt. I'll just

16

be able to show him what I learned next June." She turned toward the mantle clock over the fireplace. It was only 10:15. Plenty of time to write home.

# CHAPTER 2

*"I hope you're minding your manners,"* her mother's most recent letter admonished. *"I know they have a lot of servants, but you can always do a little extra besides taking care of Alexandra."*

Marcy smiled to herself as she brushed her teeth before bed. If only her mother knew what it was that her employer asked of her. And it wasn't all that bad, either. She could just imagine telling her mother about her secret meeting with Mr. Van Couvering, all in the name of being cooperative. She nodded complacently, hugging her arms to her chest in remembrance. In fact, she'd thought about him almost exclusively in the five days that had passed. For he hadn't been back. He'd been in Paris on business.

She frowned and toyed with the hem of her skirt. It was wrong, she knew, to have engaged in that behavior with someone besides Kurt. They had promised their love to each other, and that implied faithfulness. How could she have done it so readily with her new employer when, for a year, she wouldn't let Kurt touch most of her? Even she didn't know the answers to these questions.

Perhaps she could blame it on her new frame of mind: coming east for experience. Yet, that didn't ring true, for never in her wildest imaginings of this year, when she had sat in the rocking chair in the corner of her bedroom, had an encounter as she had just experienced entered her mind.

But, despite these unanswered, troubling questions, and the vague promise she'd made to herself not to do that again, she had a nagging fear that she'd never be able to endure a year without doing it again. It had been too thrilling not to try it at least once more. Anyway, what harm could come of doing it with Mr. Van Couvering again? It would be like an old friend. If he were to ask her again.

Marcy shook her head, blotting out these intrusive thoughts. In truth, she didn't know what to do. She only knew that she relived that night over and over, and that she tingled each time.

But Mr. Van Couvering was gone to some fabulous part of Paris, so it didn't really matter anyway. She pressed her thighs together again, feeling them moisten at the mere thought of his long, sinewy body on top of hers.

She slipped into her long-sleeved cotton nightie, stretched and clambered into bed, for a day of swimming and making strawberry jam with Alexandra had somehow been tiring. And tomorrow, at last, she'd meet Alexandra's friend and the *au pair*, Giselle, from Paris. Maybe Giselle and Mr. Van Couvering had passed each other on the metro and never known it, she mused whimsically.

Marcy looked forward to meeting her; she

19

needed some adult company. Although she had no idea what the girl would really be like, what she did know of her seemed likable: she'd been here for the past six months, her English was flawless, she had great energy, was fun and kind.

Sighing, Marcy fluffed up her pillow and lay down, looking forward to tomorrow.

Now she stood next to Giselle, with her short-cropped hair and lithe body, each pushing her little girl on a swing, part of the many contraptions of the Van Couvering climbing set.

"You must meet my friends," Giselle said, brushing her hair backward. She glanced at Marcy. "We know lots of boys, too, from the University."

Marcy returned the look, guiltily. Did it show? Could Giselle tell? Was there some sign that proclaimed, "Not a virgin?" But Giselle remained impassive to Marcy's look.

"I'd like that. I've been getting lonely here, especially because the Van Couverings are away a lot."

"Well, don't worry," Giselle purred, her "r's" rolling off her tongue. "Hey, are you free tomorrow night?"

Marcy nodded. She was always free after Alexandra went to bed. But usually she watched television or read or wrote letters.

"I'll pick you up and we'll go to Sigrid's. She's from Norway."

"Great. Thanks. Do you have a boyfriend?"

Marcy asked hesitantly.

"I've had a few, but I think I just found a semi-permanent one. What about you? Do you have one or want one?"

Then, suddenly, like a thunderbolt, Marcy blurted. "What about contraception? I need it. I'm afraid I'll get pregnant." She clapped her hand over her mouth, wide-eyed with shame. She hadn't even known she'd been thinking that.

Giselle smiled and put her arm around Marcy's shoulder. "Tell you what, *ma chere*. See if you can be free at 4:00 tomorrow. I'll take you to my doctor."

Marcy thanked her. It was so easy. And there was no condemnation. Just a simple helping hand. Maybe, just maybe, these things she'd done were meant to be. She slowed down the swing so Alexandra could climb off and then begin her ascent to the overhead ladder.

"Come on, Marcy," she cried, "climb with us."

Marcy nodded, and joyously climbed the ladder after the child, her pale blue skirt billowing up behind her. Giselle clapped her hands as Marcy's skirt gathered about her waist in the spring breeze.

"Ooo-la-la," she cooed.

Marcy giggled. Finally, there was someone to laugh with.

It was after 9:00 that night. She sat at the small white desk.

*"Dear Kurt. Thank you for your note. The days*

*go by so fast here, with swimming or biking. I put Alexandra on the back of a bike in a kid seat and take off for miles. I finally met someone my age, a girl from France. I think I'm going to like her. Anyway, it won't be quite as lonely as it's been. I'm off to bed now. Tell Mom I'll write tomorrow. I love you.*" Marcy drew a heart with an arrow and both their names, folded the letter and slipped it into an envelope.

She stood up, pushed the fabric chair under the desk, and lazily prepared for bed. But she stopped as she heard a light tap at the door. Who could it be? If it were Alexandra, she would have heard her rustling through the intercom.

"Yes?"

"Me," said the deep voice, as the door slowly opened.

"Oh, I didn't expect you," Marcy gasped in astonishment at the trim, tanned figure before her. She felt her heart pound with excitement.

"Apparently, my wife didn't either. She's out. No servants. No dinner."

"Can I make you some?" she burst in, remembering her mother's words.

"No, thank you. I was just hoping that at least one person would greet me upon my return from foreign waters," he laughed, his tall, elegant body framed in the doorway. He glanced around the room, his eyes resting on the sealed envelope. "Am I disturbing you?"

"No," she said hastily, "I just finished." She

smiled broadly and stepped back, as if beckoning him to join her.

Softly, Mr. Van Couvering closed the door.

Marcy's heart hammered against her breast as her gaze dropped to his pants. What, she wondered, did it really look like? She knew what it felt like inside his pants, she knew what it felt like inside her body, but what did it look like unfettered? She glanced up quickly, afraid Mr. Van Couvering would notice.

He had.

"Come, come here, Marcy," he spoke gently and reached out for her elbow, guiding her closer.

She took a slight step forward, wondering, suddenly and again, if this were right. What would she say in tomorrow's letter to her mother? That she'd read Jane Austen's books tonight and watched television and listened to crickets?

Scarcely daring to breathe, she waited as Mr. Van Couvering unfastened the three buttons of her nightie, one by one. She felt that familiar sense begin to grow within her. She pressed her thighs tightly together, to try to control it. He drew her closer and tilted her head upward to kiss her lips, parting them with his tongue.

Urgently, Marcy pressed against him and felt his hardness rise against her. She squirmed against him, all scruples abandoned as her body met his.

Lanquidly, he slipped her nightgown off her shoulders, and drew it down her slim, full bosomed body to the carpet.

"Ah, lovely," he breathed, lifting her breasts upward. He bent down to suckle them.

Marcy squeezed her eyes shut, embarrassed at her nakedness in the light. The other night had been different. He hadn't stared. He'd just felt her. But now she saw his eyes travel the curves of her large breasts with their taut dark ends, and rove over the slim hips, firm stomach and supple thighs.

She opened her eyes as Mr. Van Couvering took her sturdy hand and placed it on the top button of his shirt. She undid it carefully, trying not to crease the well-pressed cotton. Then she unfastened the next button and the others. He didn't stop her, he did nothing but run his fingers lightly over her back and her ribs and her neck.

His shirt opened, revealing well-developed pectoral muscles, covered with black hair. She caught her breath in excitement. She slid his shirt off his shoulders and onto the floor next to her nightgown and kicked the clothing away with her bare toes. She ran her hands over his chest in delight.

But a shyness overtook her, paralyzing her to go further. She knew what she wanted to do. She desperately wanted to pull at his belt, slide the button out of its hole and unzip his pants. But she couldn't. It was too alien, too dangerous.

Instead, Mr. Van Couvering removed her hands and placed one on his belt buckle. She knew what he wanted, and adroitly, she undid it. He placed his hand on top of hers so she wouldn't remove it.

He moved her fingers, giving her the sign to continue. Shyly, she unfastened his button, unzipped his zipper. His navy blue suit pants dropped to the floor.

Marcy stared in exquisite appreciation of the hearty bulge straining against the confines of his underwear. Unable to take her eyes from the giant member, she pulled at his underpants and took them to the floor.

Without thinking, she reached out and grabbed his manhood with her fingers. "Ah," she breathed deeply. "So this is it." She cocked her head to the side, examining its contours.

With trepidation, Marcy ran her fingers along the shaft, gently pulling, til he moaned and pulled her toward him. His tip pressed against her belly. She felt him grasp her from behind, kneading her firm cheeks with his fingers. She rubbed her breasts against his chest, never letting go of his member. He groaned and lay his hand on the top of her head, urging her down to her knees.

She dropped and faced his turgid member.

"Do it," he commanded gently, his hand still on her head.

Timidly, unsure of what he expected, Marcy touched the tip with her tongue. She circled it gingerly for a few moments, til she felt Mr. Van Couvering thrust himself between her lips. She opened her mouth and sucked him. Shivers raced across her body. She withdrew and took him again, then pulled back, then leaned forward gobbling him up until he could go no further.

His body stiffened.

"Come, come here," he said hoarsely, pulling her up. He led her to the double bed and placed her down amid the mountains of pillows. He straddled her, so that his manhood rested on her stomach.

Again, she fondled it. He lifted her breasts, leaned over and mouthed her til she writhed from the heat. He buried his face between them and pressed them against his cheeks. Marcy grimaced with joy as she dug her fingers into his back.

She could bear it no longer. "Now," she gasped. "Now. Do it now."

"Wait a bit," he replied, lifting his face from her body. He ran his fingers across her stomach til her gut turned.

"Now," she clenched her teeth, aching for release. Her hips arched upward, begging him to enter. Boldly, she reached for him, trying to pull him down into her, but still he would not. He only ran his fingers over her belly and ribs, while his throbbing member rested between the cavity of her breasts, glistening with sweat.

Madly, Marcy thrashed about, her legs wildly seeking an anchor.

And then, he slid down, quickly inserting his hard member. She pushed against him, but he would not be forced. With slow, rhythmic determination, he rotated himself within her, silently commanding her to tame her passion. Then, he began to move faster, guiding her movements by his stabs. Faster and faster they hammered against each other. And then the explosive passion came, waves upon waves of flashing heat til she was spent.

Panting, she threw her head back against the pillows, exhausted. She let his perfumed sweat waft over her.

"Welcome back, Mr. Van Couvering," she blushed.

Mr. Van Couvering looked down at her and smiled. "You are a delight, Marcy."

"Really?" She giggled, unhindered by shame. "I guess if you're going to do something, you might as well do it right."

He sat up and dressed rapidly. Marcy didn't move. Instead, she lay against the pillows, her shining hair spread about her, excited by her discoveries and pleased with herself for a job well-done.

"Good night, Marcy," Mr. Van Couvering waved and sauntered out the door. "I hope you'll forgive my running like this."

"Sure, no problem, sir," she smiled. And it wasn't a problem. He was, after all, her employer. Luxuriously, she stretched out and fell asleep til morning.

Alexandra woke her early the next day, for they planned a breakfast picnic. Quickly, they dressed and tiptoed down the back staircase past the servants' quarters.

"What shall we have?" Marcy grinned at the girl. "Muffins? Milk? Fruit?"

Alexandra nodded to each of these and Marcy busied herself pulling them from the shelves and the frig and packing them in a large wooden picnic hamper. As she reached for some napkins, a hand stopped her movement.

She turned eagerly, expecting to see Mr. Van Couvering.

Instead, Mrs. Van Couvering faced her. Her hair and makeup were immaculate. Her white satin robe glimmered in the haze of the new morning.

"Oh, you scared me," Marcy swallowed nervously. She'd scarcely talked to Mrs. Van Couvering. What could she want, especially at 7:00 in the morning? But, even before she asked herself that question, she knew the answer. Mrs. Van Couvering had heard the two of them last night. She had returned home while he was in her room. She had heard the moans, heard the bed rustling under their eager movements. Marcy's heart froze.

"Good morning, Marcy," she said softly, her brown eyes sparkling in her pale face. "I think we should have a little talk."

Marcy bit her lip. "About what?" she managed.

"I think you might know." Mrs. Van Couvering turned toward Alexandra in the kitchen. "How about tomorrow morning at nine or so in the sunroom?"

"Please, ma'am, could you tell me now?" Marcy

28

was stricken with terror. This was the end. She would lose her job and return, in disgrace, to High Flats. What would she tell her mother and Kurt? How could she face her family? For, surely, they would know, they would see it written on her face. They'd see she was fired, and they would know precisely why. Perhaps she could get another job someplace in the east for the rest of the year, and then they'd never know.

But, as Marcy turned away from the cabinets, she knew she was troubled by more. It wasn't just the disgrace she'd face. She simply wasn't ready to return to High Flats. She wasn't ready to end her life at eighteen, especially since she sensed it was truly beginning. She didn't want that lake where the bull frogs mated, the country store, the Little League baseball games and pot luck suppers just yet. She didn't want five kids now.

"Could—could—" she began.

"Not now," Mrs. Van Couvering spoke preemptorily.

"When?"

"As I said a few moments ago, tomorrow at nine in my sunroom." Mrs. Van Couvering smiled brightly. "The sun streams in there in the morning, making it a lovely setting for absolutely everything."

Marcy nodded dully at the significance of those words. Mrs. Van Couvering either wanted to underscore the cruelty of the punishment by the loveliness of the surroundings, or else hoped to soften it. Either way, Marcy didn't think she could bear the tension til then.

She felt as if she'd been ripped apart. Yes, it was true that last night and the first night with Mr. Van Couvering had been wonderful, but now, in light of this, she fervently wished they'd never happened. She rubbed her hand across her eyes, wiping away the sudden vision she had of Mr. Van Couvering riding her chest with his hard member perched between her breasts. She could taste him, smell him. And she didn't want to.

Mrs. Van Couvering turned on her velveted heel and, blowing a kiss to her daughter, sailed out of the kitchen.

Marcy leaned weakly against the counter.

"What's the matter, Marcy? Let's go." Alexandra tugged at her skirt.

Numbly, Marcy stood upright. It would do no good for the little girl to know that this was her last day here. Tears filled her eyes as she snapped the picnic hamper shut and routinely took Alexandra's hand in her own as they walked out the back door to the veranda and onto the verdant lawn.

Alexandra chirped the morning away and Marcy was grateful, for she could scarcely attend. A great pain lodged in the pit of her stomach. Finally, toward noon, they returned to the house so Alexandra could nap.

"How was the picnic, Alexandra?" Theresa, the cook, asked as Marcy lay the hamper on the steel counter.

"Great. Only Marcy forgot the napkins, so I had to use my sweatshirt." Alexandra pointed to the red strawberry stain on the edge of her clothing.

"We'll get it out, don't you fear," Theresa said fondly. She turned to Marcy. "You still want me to watch her this afternoon while you go out with Giselle?"

Marcy clapped her hand over her mouth. She'd forgotten. Those plans to visit Giselle's doctor seemed to have been made so long ago. And they seemed pointless now. But how could she cancel at so late a date, especially when Giselle had been so kind? Anyway, she'd probably need contraception at some time in her life, so she might as well get it over with now.

"Yes, thanks, Theresa." She smiled wanly.

She took Alexandra up for her nap and bent over, tousling her hair. It would be their last nap together. "Sleep well, pumpkin. See you later." Marcy smiled miserably. She wouldn't have dinner with Giselle, for she wanted to spend the last few hours with Alexandra.

Unthinkingly, she returned to her room and opened her bureau drawers, pulling out her skirts and blouses and placing them on the bed. From the closet, she withdrew her heavy black vinyl suitcase and placed it on the floor. Leadenly, she placed her clothes inside, and drew the straps across them to hold them in place. She'd do her toilet articles, such as they were, later.

"The first thing," whispered Giselle confidentially the first minute they were together, "is the gyno for some sort of contraception. She'll discuss your choices and you can pick one."

Mechanically, Marcy nodded. She'd said nothing of her impending meeting with Mrs. Van Couvering, and tried to look excited. Then, like a bolt, an idea flashed. Perhaps Giselle would know of somewhere else she could work. Someone else who would want her. Only this time, she'd make sure there was no Mr. Van Couvering to enter her life.

Buoyed, she turned happily to her new friend. She wouldn't bring it up now. She'd wait til tomorrow. At the very least, Giselle could help her find a job at a fast food restaurant or clothing store. Or something. Confident that her plan would work, Marcy climbed into Giselle's Firebird and headed for the doctor.

An hour later, she was a new woman, outfitted with a contraceptive device, her protection from some of the ravages of an unknown future. She no longer cared to return immediately to the Van Couverings and Alexandra. She felt a tug of freedom from the weight that had dampened her all day. She'd see Alexandra in the morning.

They walked to a Chinese restaurant where Sigrid met them. Immediately, Marcy knew she'd like both young women and felt that, between them, she'd find employment. They giggled over egg drop soup and moo sho pork and told about

32

themselves over fortune cookies and Jasmine tea.

"Me?" Sigrid smiled, her white-blonde hair hanging halfway down her back. "I'm from a small Norwegian town. I have an older brother who's a doctor. My parents are both doctors. I'll spend the year here and then go back to college."

"What'll you study?" Marcy asked, breaking open her cookie. Vaguely, she wished she had the hunger for more education.

"Anatomy."

"She's got a head start," Giselle giggled.

Sigrid and Marcy joined her. But behind her laughter, Marcy wondered how Sigrid appeared so normal if, in fact, she was so—industrious.

"We'll get you started, too," Giselle nudged Marcy.

Marcy shifted uncomfortably. Was it so obvious? Why did everyone seem to have a critical opinion about sexual prowess? Some people thought it was forbidden, and others thought it was mandatory.

She turned toward Giselle. "How about you? What's your history?"

"Ah, not much. I'm from Paris. My mama is a housewife, my papa an engineer. I have a brother, one year younger, 18."

"How long will you be here?" Suddenly, she was afraid of the loneliness when Giselle and Sigrid would leave.

"Ah, another year or so. I love it."

Marcy nodded with pleasure. "Oh, look at my fortune. 'Work hard to achieve greatness.' Wonder what it could be?"

"I once had, 'Wash face in morning and neck at night,'" Sigrid bubbled with laughter.

"I'd like them a little spicier, frankly," Marcy grumbled in mock irritation.

The girls chatted til closing and then Giselle dropped Marcy home. "We'll have fun." She leaned over and kissed Marcy lightly on either cheek, in the French manner. "I'm glad you've come to join us."

"Me, too. And I love the way you say my name with that cute little 'r' sound." Marcy opened the car door. "Oh, and thanks for my new—thing," she added delicately.

Beaming, she raced up the front steps to the house, filled with happy remembrances of the day. Then with a thud, she recalled the morning. All her evening's joy vanished and that leaden stone in her stomach returned. She turned toward the stairs but stopped as she heard voices from behind the closed library door.

Their voices. But, though she strained, she couldn't hear what they said.

"Is that you, Marcy?" Mr. Van Couvering called out affably.

"Yes, sir," she replied meekly as the heavy wooden door opened. She dropped her eyes in shame.

But what she really wanted to do was race into that room, pound her fists against his chest over and over until they were bruised. He had done this to her. He had made her love her job and her future here, and then he had ruined her. Tears filled her eyes as she sadly climbed the winding staircase to her room.

Tomorrow she would be gone. If he cared, he would have come to the steps to bid her good-night. But he made it clear. He wanted no further involvement. Chest heaving, as she tried to contain her sobs, she raced down the hallway to her room to cry in peace.

# CHAPTER 3

The time had come. It was 9:00. Marcy had dropped Alexandra off at summer camp, and waved gaily to Giselle who was dropping off Jessica, hoping to dispel her own mood of doom. She returned, fearfully, to the Van Couverings.

As Lawrence drove through the iron gates, up the long tree-shrouded drive, her presentiment of disaster grew stronger. For this would be it.

Mrs. Van Couvering obviously had not wanted Alexandra to witness her sad departure, for she had left a note in Marcy's room the previous night reminding her to present herself in the sunroom. As if she could forget, Marcy thought ruefully.

And now Marcy sat, unmoving in the back of the car as it edged up the drive. Drawing a deep breath, she opened the car door without waiting for Lawrence, a custom she had not yet acquired, and headed for the flagstone steps.

The front door opened as she touched the iron handle. Mrs. Van Couvering, dressed in white tennis outfit and sneakers, stood before her.

"Please, come in, Marcy," she said in her soft voice. She led Marcy to her sunroom, a room Marcy had never been in. It was off the main hall, in its own private cul-de-sac. It was airy, light,

36

painted pristine white with bright green and yellow accents of spring and summer.

Scarcely daring to look up from her feet, clad in the sensible black pumps from High Flats, Marcy noticed the small, ladylike desk, a wide wicker couch and a few wicker arm chairs scattered about the intimate room. Vertical blinds hung down. They were shut. Marcy shuddered. Would Mrs. Van Couvering flog her also?

The petite mistress closed the door. "For privacy," she smiled.

Marcy dared to smile back, but only fleetingly. She wanted to show her good grace. For she knew she'd been wrong. What she wanted to do was fall to her knees and beg for forgiveness and promise never to do it again. But it was unforgiveable. She had fornicated with a married man, this woman's husband. Tremulously, she swallowed.

"Marcy," the voice was so low that Marcy had to strain to hear it. "Marcy, I think I frightened you. I didn't mean to."

Marcy nodded glumly, blinking away tears. She wished Mrs. Van Couvering would hurry and get it over with. She couldn't bear the kindness. She held her gaze on Mrs. Van Couvering's well-formed slight calves, ready for tennis.

"I saw your suitcase, packed."

"Yes, ma'am."

"I spoke too abruptly, I'm afraid. I'm not sure why."

For a moment, Marcy's hope was pricked.

"No one should ever speak so harshly. I suppose I was just preoccupied."

Marcy nodded again, not quite following the conversational line.

"Marcy." Mrs. Van Couvering walked toward her, a full two inches shorter. She lifted her hand and held it upright as if stopping a car at an intersection. "I saw you making love with my husband."

Marcy gasped. Saw! This was worse than she imagined. "Don't you mean heard?"

"No," Mrs. Van Couvering replied simply. "Saw. I saw him enter your room the other night, the night I was out. I came home early. I was at the top of the stairs when he knocked and entered your room."

Marcy waited, a frantic sense of terror welling. She waited for more, and silently begged the woman to hurry and announce the punishment.

"Then I tiptoed down the hall to your door."

Hurry, hurry, Marcy screamed silently.

"I watched through the keyhole. The whole thing, from beginning to end." She stared straight at Marcy.

Marcy reeled backward against the wicker chair. This was far worse than she had imagined. She'd seen them, she'd heard them. Would this torture never end? Why did she review it so slowly? Wide-eyed, her gut twisting, she waited as Mrs. Van Couvering continued.

"I saw my husband mount you. I saw you take

him with your mouth."

Marcy's jaw dropped open, too shocked to even think. For never did she imagine that her activities had been catalogued. She groaned inwardly. Now what? Would Mrs. Van Couvering write the employment agency? Would the agency write her mother? She couldn't move. Her will had eroded.

"I want you to do that with me." Mrs. Van Couvering said evenly. "I think I would like it very much." She stopped a moment. "Would that appeal to you? My husband thinks I would like it also."

Gasping, Marcy groped for the table top next to her so she could stand. What was Mrs. Van Couvering *talking* about? Do what *exactly* to her? How could she do the same things she'd done with Mr. Van Couvering to a *woman?* What was she supposed to touch? How was she supposed to do it? Marcy felt sudden nausea grow within her at the thought of a woman's body. And what would Mrs. Van Couvering do to *her?*

Marcy clenched her teeth together to try to quell the nausea. The very idea horrified her. Would Mrs. Van Couvering kiss her lips and her body as Mr. Van Couvering had done? How would they mount each other? How would they make each other come? Was it even possible? Marcy shook her head in bewilderment.

"No, I don't think so, ma'am," she whispered hoarsely, barely able to speak. "I've never heard of anything like this. I wouldn't even know what to do."

"I could show you," Mrs. Van Couvering answered softly, reaching out for Marcy's hand. But Marcy stepped back, shaking her head from side to side.

"I'm not sure I would like it. I think it would be—" she searched for a word. "Weird. I don't think we're supposed to do something like this."

"Mr. Van Couvering mentioned that you might be hesitant. He suggested that I remind you that this touching is just a way two people become closer."

Marcy nodded. Tears welled in her eyes. He had used those very words to her, and they had made sense then. But now? She didn't know. It didn't seem right. She cast a sidelong glance at Mrs. Van Couvering. She certainly was attractive and nice. But, ugh. Unwittingly, Marcy's face scrunched up in distaste as she thought of the repulsive touching they would do together.

It was disgusting. She had never heard of women doing it together. A slight moan escaped her. How could this be happening? How did she get thrust into this awful situation? Wasn't this a *sin?*

And wouldn't it be additionally disloyal and cruel to Kurt to have sex with a woman? Even if she finally did it, how could she ever hide such a thing from her mother and him?

If the wrath of the Heavens had not rained down upon her before with her activities with Mr.

Van Couvering, they surely would now. If she had successfully deceived her mother and Kurt thus far, she surely would fail now. She would feel horribly dirty forever. And somehow the filth would seep into the letters home like grime under your fingernails that you could never, no matter how hard you tried, scrape out.

Marcy stared, open-mouthed. "Oh, Mrs. Van Couvering, I—" She stopped. What if she didn't do what Mrs. Van Couvering asked? What if Mr. Van Couvering found out that she hadn't done it with his wife? There would be no possibility of saving her job if they both detested her. Surely, she would get fired. Was it worse to be fired or kiss and hug and touch another woman? A thousand conflicting, horrifying thoughts swirled within.

And then it dawned on her. Did this mean she wouldn't be fired? Did this mean that Mrs. Van Couvering had never intended to lower the axe, that she had only wanted to lure Marcy into her sunroom? "Why, then, don't I just jump at the chance to save myself?" she wondered in bewilderment. "What happens if I just put all my hesitations aside and do it for the sake of staying in the east?"

A ray of hope cheered her: her job was safe . . . but was the alternative something she could do? It was so forbidden, so repulsive to her very soul and the souls of all those whom she held dear.

And yet, she was about to be saved from the ignominy of returning home a fallen, failed woman. Saved from the embarrassment of seeking help from Giselle or Sigrid.

"It's a simple request. Mr. Van Couvering is aware of it." Mrs. Van Couvering reached out for Marcy's hand and lifted it to her lips. She kissed the palm softly and ran her lips around the curves where the fingers met the palm. Still silently, she placed Marcy's hand on her small breasts. Marcy felt the nipples already poised. But still she could not react. She stood paralyzed with the unfamiliar feeling of touching a woman's breast.

She felt as if she had suddenly become a man. She didn't *want* to feel this woman's nipples. She wrinkled her nose at the sudden terrifying thought: what happened if she had to touch her—her private parts? She swallowed nervously, and let Mrs. Van Couvering run one hand over Marcy's shoulders and hips, while the other still pressed Marcy's palm to her breast.

With her own hand covering Marcy's, Mrs. Van Couvering massaged the girl's palm firmly against her flesh so that Marcy felt the softness move beneath her hand. Then, despite herself, Marcy shifted her hand slightly and found that her fingers lay against the other woman's hard tips. But, still, she did not move her body any further.

Then, surprisingly, as she stood dumbly wondering how to proceed, as Mrs. Van Couvering gently ran her soft fingers over her curves, Marcy felt herself moisten.

"Oh, beautiful," murmured Mrs. Van Couvering as she skimmed her free hand over Marcy's bosom and hips. Then she hitched up her own shoulder, dropping one side of her tennis dress to reveal her breast. She hitched the other. The dress dropped free. Mrs. Van Couvering wore no bra. Marcy removed her hand and stared at the most perfectly shaped breasts. They tilted upward, their ends pointed as if in welcome.

With sudden surprise, Marcy felt her heart begin beating harder and her breath come faster.

"Yes, Marcy, yes," Mrs. Van Couvering whispered. "It's OK. Yes."

Marcy stared in amazement at the other woman's beauty. Mrs. Van Couvering lifted one of Marcy's hands and placed it on her bosom. Marcy's loins turned with unforeseen, unexpected excitement.

She sighed with delight. Why, this wasn't awful at all. Somehow, the gut-wrenching thoughts of before were suddenly buried as she touched the woman in front of her. Without a second thought, she cast her doubts aside as that tingling began to invade her.

Suddenly it didn't seem to matter whose body would be next to hers. What mattered was only that their bodies would be together. She cupped Mrs. Van Couvering's breasts and gently pawed at them as Mr. Van Couvering had done to her. She bent down and licked the hard points. Surprised, she found she liked this. It wasn't the slightest bit grotesque at all. It was as wonderful as it had been with Mr. Van Couvering.

Mrs. Van Couvering guided Marcy to the floor. Swiftly, she pulled Marcy's shirt from her skirt, reached around and skillfully unfastened her skirt. She lifted them off.

"What lovely, full breasts, Marcy." She lunged at them with her fingers, kneading them, wrapping them around her own cheeks, licking them.

Marcy gasped with pleasure, the same sort she'd had with this woman's husband. But now, as she succumbed to the unwavering heat, she no longer cared whether a man or a woman had her, or precisely how well they knew one another.

Marcy ran her hand along the contours of Mrs. Van Couvering's back and felt her arch with expectation. She felt Mrs. Van Couvering drop her fingers into her cotton underpants til she found her mound. Mrs. Van Couvering rolled on top of Marcy so they could simultaneously fondle each other's bodies with their hands and mouths in a delicious eagerness.

Marcy felt Mrs. Van Couvering knowledgeably probe the sensitive spots of her vulva, and she copied the gestures as if she were a schoolgirl with a teacher. She heard herself and her teacher groan with delight as they feverishly explored each other's bodies.

Through heavy-lidded eyes, she saw droplets of sun pushing against the closed blinds and imagined the blazing light shining on them as they kissed each other. As she languidly caressed the other woman's smooth flesh and felt her push against her body, she was suddenly surprised to feel Mrs. Van Couvering wriggle around, her legs sliding into the position that her head had been in.

But then, she knew. She felt the unfamiliar tongue thrust deep into her own cavity. Marcy responded in the same fashion. She squealed as the tongue lashed harder and faster against her even as they rode each other harder. And then, arching toward one another, they came, their tongues working together, replacing the well-known husband.

Exhausted, the shame expunged, Marcy's head lay on top of Mrs. Van Couvering's thigh, her face glistening with sweat. Lazily, she ran her fingers on the woman's inner leg, feeling the soft flesh quiver.

"What did you think?" Mrs. Van Couvering asked, still breathless.

"Very nice, very, very nice," Marcy panted back. "But the best part is that I'm not going to get fired."

"Fired?" Mrs. Van Couvering sat up. "Why would you think that?"

"From what you said yesterday morning," Marcy answered. "I was so afraid. It probably made this even better."

"Then I'll have to scare you every time." She pulled her tennis dress up and pulled up her silk panties. "My husband was right."

Marcy looked at her quizzically.

"You need different underclothes." Mrs. Van Couvering patted her shoulder. "I've got to hurry. I have to meet the pro."

Marcy stared after the petite woman as she left the room. She stood, stretched her long, strong limbs and pulled her schoolgirlish clothes on. Puzzled, she wondered to whom she belonged? The little girl, Alexandra? The master? The wife? Her parents and Kurt? Suddenly, the placidity that had overtaken her, receded, as, horrified, she realized what she had just done. Now, more than ever, she felt as if she had truly sinned. And yet—and yet, it felt so natural, so good. How in the world could she ever explain this to Kurt? Not just a man, but with his wife?

Unexpectedly, Marcy giggled. It was all so awful, so tawdry, that it was laughable. Giselle would love it. But she better not tell her. Who knew what gossip could destroy her? Better not to think about this. She'd just write Kurt and her mother as if she were the same Marcy who'd left High Flats. Only now it appeared as if she had a new hobby.

Marcy leaned over to put the ends of the white rug back in place. Then, she too, left the room to fetch Alexandra at camp.

When Marcy returned with Alexandra later that day, a large package, gaily wrapped in yellow and turquoise, lay on her bed next to her still-packed suitcase. Eagerly, she tore off the wrapper, not knowing what to expect.

"Ohh," she breathed, as she pulled out six pairs of silk bikini underwear.

She held the bikinis to her, admiring the delicate lace waist and thigh bands. Three were black, three white. She spied six tiny bras nestled among the tissue paper, like puppies nursing against their mother. Surely, the cups would not cover her generous breasts. She scooped up one.

Quickly, she pulled off her blouse and stalwart cotton bra and put on a black one. It fit. At least it fit the bottom part of her breast and covered her nipple. But the top part of flesh was exposed. Mountains of flesh. What in the world would Kurt say when he felt it? Or her mother when she saw it dangling from the laundry rack in the bathroom? Ah, well, it wouldn't ever be worn in High Flats.

Carefully, knowing she'd wear it again at the end of this year, Marcy took her own, old bra and placed it in the suitcase, along with the others she had packed for home. For while she would remove the clothes that she had packed last night and hang them back in the closet and fold them back into drawers, her underwear would remain the hard-backed suitcase, waiting for High Flats.

But the vinyl suitcase wouldn't remain unused for very long.

For Mr. and Mrs. Van Couvering had summoned her and Alexandra to join them at their home in Paris for the holidays. Now, having packed Alexandra's suitcase and put the child to bed, she attended to her own.

The summer months had lazily wafted into early, then late fall. She and Mr. Van Couvering joyously met each other in many of the late nights that he was in town. Mrs. Van Couvering frequently summoned her to the sunroom in the morning light. And now it was pressing close to Christmas. They would celebrate with parties in Paris. How elegant.

Marcy shivered with anticipation: the anticipation of foreign places and enticing sex. She desperately wanted both.

She hadn't seen her master and mistress in the many weeks since they had gone to Europe for the social season and his business. They called Alexandra at least once daily and sent her gifts of toys or clothes or flowers every few days. But they were absent. And Alexandra and Marcy missed them.

Now, of course, it wasn't dreadfully lonely, since she had Giselle and Sigrid and their friends to dine and party with. But there was a distinct absence in her life. For, aside from the gaiety, she'd been alone. No one had attracted her either physically or mentally, as she found herself thinking almost entirely of Mr. Van Couvering and occasionally of Mrs. Van Couvering. Although Giselle urged her to come out of her shell more, Marcy's attention was devotedly fixed on her employer.

Silly, she knew, but she couldn't help it. She'd been thinking of him since that last fiery night. There'd been a knock at the door late at night.

" 'Tis I," said the well-known voice. The door opened silently. Mr. Van Couvering strode in, still dressed in his gray pinstripe suit pants, starched white shirt and red diamond-pattern tie. Only his jacket was off.

"Ah, Marcy, I hope I didn't disturb you. I came to say goodbye. We'll be leaving early in the morning." He stood by the door.

"Thank you for coming." Marcy sat up against the pillows where she'd been writing Kurt. "Don't worry. Everything will be under control." She struggled to her feet and walked over to him. Her thick golden hair framed her healthy face as she smiled, aware of a heat flashing through her.

As if to quell it, she put her arm out to shake his. He grabbed it, gently pulling her to him. He leaned over slightly as she tipped her head back so their lips could meet. Suddenly, seized by a violence she'd not felt before, she lunged against his body, throwing him back against the wall. Frantically, she reached for the zipper of his pants and tugged it down, even as she wriggled against him.

"Not so fast, little one," he whispered into her ear, as his hands groped for her breasts under her flannel nightie.

But she wouldn't wait. Desperately, a ferocious passion suffusing her limbs, she gripped his member and lifted it from his pants. She could not stop. She rubbed her fingers on it, feeling it rise within her grasp. And then, without a moment's

49

hesitation, she stood on tiptoes, hiked up her nightgown, and guided him within her.

"I need it now," she pleaded, vigorously pushing against him.

She threw herself against him wildly, until her strength was sapped, her body spent. She hadn't bothered to think of him. What had he felt? Had he enjoyed it? Had she done her job? Tonight, it had not mattered. She had done what she needed, precisely when she'd needed it.

Exhausted she lay against him, until she felt his member grow softer. She extricated herself, giggling. A vague feeling of unease gnawed at her. For the first time in the many weeks he had taken her, she hadn't bothered to perform for him. Would he be angry?

Mr. Van Couvering replaced his organ in his pants nonchalantly.

"I'm sorry," Marcy mumbled. "I really wasn't very considerate."

"But, Marcy, none of this is wrong. It is natural, it is right. Nothing between us is bad." He put his arm around her shoulders. "Please, there is nothing wrong you can do in the household as long as my child is well taken care of."

Marcy looked up gratefully.

"Truly," he nodded, kissing her cheek. "And now, off to bed." Mr. Van Couvering lifted his fingers in a wave and left the room.

She stared at the closing door remorsefully.

Even as she thought about her own behavior,

aggressively reaching for a man, she was ashamed. Oh well, she thought, I'll just have to forget it, and not do it again.

She retreated to the pillows and picked up the pen to resume her letter to Kurt. ". . . *giraffes and elephants,*" she continued.

Lazily, she let her fingers drift to her vulva which she tenderly touched in recollection of the final moments with Mr. Van Couvering. *"Mr. and Mrs. Van Couvering depart tomorrow for Paris for five or six weeks or so. Alexandra and I will probably join them. I can't wait. I miss you, Kurt, and hope you think of me as I think of you."*

As she thought of his strong, bull-like body, so different from the manicured one of Mr. Van Couvering, her fingers wandered deeper in expectation of seeing Kurt in the spring, trying to come — in vain.

But now, shaking her head to erase those memories, Marcy knew she'd better hurry and pack or she'd be up all night. She folded her navy pleated skirt on top of the grey and black ones, placed her cotton blouses on the left next to a couple sweaters, and then on top, she carefully placed her lace panties and bras.

She couldn't wait. At the very least she'd see Mr. Van Couvering and be rid of that omnivorous lust that gripped her incessantly. It forced her almost nightly trying to bring herself to climax. She found her fingers poised on the edge of her vulva, exploring, touching, caressing herself. And yet,

strangely, she was left unsatisfied, still hungering.
Now it was time to do something about it.

# CHAPTER 4

Marcy gripped Alexandra's hand tightly as they left the plane. How in the world would she ever figure out where their luggage was, she wondered nervously. What if no one spoke English? How would she find the Van Couverings? What was she, an 18-year-old, who hardly spoke high school French, doing here anyway? Alexandra returned the pressure.

"Madamoiselle Marcy?"

Marcy jerked, finding herself looking into the green eyes of a young man, her height.

"M. Van Couvering has asked me to escort you through customs," he spoke English flawlessly. "*Bon jour*, Alexandra," he knelt down and took Alexandra's hand. "I am Daniel Guimard, M. Van Couvering's assistant.

"*Bon jour, monsieur*," Alexandra replied with a perfect accent. She curtsied.

Marcy, still clutching the child's hand, felt easier as they followed this handsome, well-built man toward their luggage and through customs.

"Daddy! Mommy!" Alexandra cried, breaking away from Marcy as she ran toward her parents. "I love you. I miss you!" She jumped into her father's arms. He hoisted her up and held her near.

"I missed you, dear one," he whispered.

Mrs. Van Couvering covered her daughter with her arms. "Never again, Alexandra. It's been too long." Together, the three walked through the throngs milling about the Charles De Gaulle Airport. Marcy, forgotten, tagged at their heels with the green-eyed man with the light brown hair.

"M. has asked that I help you meet people here and that I entertain you until you feel comfortable," he offered.

She swallowed nervously, grateful not to be excluded. "Thank you. I have some people to call. But I would be most happy to spend time with you also."

For she didn't know what those phone calls would hold for her. Giselle had given her a few names. At the top of the list was her 18-year-old brother, Yves, and then a few girlfriends. Giselle had told her to call her brother immediately since he spoke English expertly and could show her around. Somehow, though, 18 seemed so young these days. She threw a glance at Mr. Van Couvering's lean, sinewy back and Mrs. Van Couvering's petitely sculpted body.

The chauffeured Peugeot was waiting in front of the airport, clearly in an exalted position. Marcy wondered what Mr. Van Couvering did that he could command so much attention. Silently, still ignored, she was squeezed into the front seat between the chauffeur and Daniel, as the Van

Couverings climbed into the back for the hour-long ride along the Autoroute du Nord into the city.

She gasped, astounded, as she eyed the stone mansion, situated in the middle of the city, overlooking a precious little park. The house had been in Mr. Van Couvering's family for centuries, he said. "My mother's," he added, as the chauffeur opened the back door for him. "A beauty, isn't it? Wish we could spend more time here."

Perhaps it was the French ambiance or the excitement of something new, but somehow the house seemed much more imposing than their Delaware home. With its stone work, mansard roof and unceasing series of rooms, Marcy thought she would never stop gaping and gasping at its beauty.

*"Dear Mother and Dad, you wouldn't believe it. It overlooks a private garden, just for residents of this area. Even at this time of year, you can tell it's wonderful. The shrubs are pruned evenly and they always seem to come in pairs. I wish you were here. The house itself is beautiful with brocade drapes and antique furniture all over. I'm afraid to touch anything. I love you."*

And to Kurt, she wrote, *"My room is twice as large as my room at home,"* even though he'd never seen her room at home. *"It has real Louis Quartorze furniture and overlooks a small back-yard. Alexandra's room is next to mine, connected by a marble bathroom. I miss you. We'll be here til after New Year's."*

Marcy peered around her room as she joyously unpacked. She jumped at the knock on her door. "Yes?" She hoped against hope that Mr. Van Couvering had come to see her.

"Madamoiselle?" a little voice asked. "A letter."

"For me!" Marcy threw open her door to pluck it off the silver tray, carried by a black-garbed maid. It was unfamiliar writing and postmarked Paris.

*"Dear Marcy,"* it said in a masculine scrawl, *"my sister Giselle said you would arrive today, and asked me to show you around. Please call me at this number when you have a few free moments. I look forward to meeting you."* It was signed, *Yves.*

Marcy squealed for joy! It was starting! Paris! The lights and bustle of Paris. "Is there a phone?" she asked the maid who still stood at the door.

*"Oui,"* she nodded pointing to one at the end of a hall next to a high-backed, heavily carved, brocaded chair.

"Could you help me place a call?" Marcy showed the maid the phone number and asked her to ask for Yves.

"Hallo?" A male voice answered.

"Hello. Yves? This is Marcy."

"Ohh, Mar-cie, I have waited for your call."

They spoke a few minutes and agreed to meet the following evening when Alexandra was in bed.

And now it was evening. Marcy sat in the darkened library by herself waiting. No one was about.

56

She was dressed in her black pleated skirt, a light blue pull-over sweater and her black pumps and black stockings. What would he be like, Giselle's brother? Funny and dark-haired like his sister? Probably tall. She said he was very handsome.

Marcy grinned as she remembered Giselle's wink, promising more. It would be fun to have a good laugh and meet some young French people. A terrible thought clutched her. What if they didn't speak English? Then, she might as well be in a bottle cast about on the ocean.

Marcy started at the sound of the doorbell chiming throughout the house. It was he. Her heart thudded. She hadn't had a date since Kurt. She walked into the hall and then stopped, staring at a handsome young man standing before her. He was tall and lanky and dark like Giselle, almost a storybook character in his beauty. Never had she seen a more handsome man with wide shoulders, tapering chest, slim hips. A shock of black hair fell into his forehead.

Shyly, for she suddenly knew she was no match in her schoolgirl clothes and her middling experience for this man, she stuck out her hand in greeting. He leaned over, lifting it to his lips.

"I am very pleased to meet you, Marcy."

And, truly, as she glanced tremulously at him, she thought she was also.

He ushered her to the front door, carefully held her coat and led her to the steps of the mansion.

Dinner was charming in a little cafe near

Sacre-Coeur. Then, he led her through the area, up steep stone steps to open terraces, past people paying homage in the church and party-goers. Yves, taking her arm within his, walked along the Boulevard de Clichy, past more restaurants, cinemas and nightclubs. He nodded toward the Deux-Anes Theatre, promising to take her to a cabaret.

"Look," Marcy pointed. "Moulin Rouge." She grinned excitedly, thrilled to see the actual building that Toulouse-Lautrec had painted. Her parents hung a copy in their living room. "I don't think I'll ever tire of this. You know," she turned to Yves, eagerly, "I've never been in a big city for any length of time before. Mostly, a day or two somewhere, like New York or Philadelphia or Chicago." She squeezed his arm with hers. "This is fabulous."

They kept walking, the brisk air dogging their footsteps. Yves explained some of the history of the area, inviting her to join him again for other tours. Marcy smiled happily, aware that the night was fleeting, but happy with the city, and content with him.

He was clearly knowledgeable and bright. He had a gentleness that she admired. Several times, as they sauntered near the Place du Tertre, he stopped to greet friends, also ambling by or strutting with great determination to an unknown destination. They spoke in English in her behalf so that she felt included.

"In the summer," Yves said, "this is so crowded

with people and lights and artists painting that you can hardly get by. But it is late. Do you want to go back, or stay out some more? There is so much for us to do together."

Did she imagine it, or had he blown into her ear as he said that? For, unexpectedly, she felt herself quicken. Embarrassed, as if he could see, she leaned against the side of an old brick building and clamped her legs tightly together, as if to stop the turmoil just beginning.

He leaned down and kissed her lightly on the lips. Marcy replied hungrily—for it had been so long—and opened them as he thrust his tongue deeply into the darkness of her mouth. He squirmed against her. Her pulse raced as she felt him, even through their winter coats. But what could they do here? How far would he take this?

"No, I don't think so," she stammered, pushing him away with her hands on his chest. "Not now, not here." For something told her that if she didn't stop here and now, there would be no stopping. She relished the release and she hungered for this man before her. "Let's—let's see something." For, where could they go? She broke away and pressed her hand against her hammering heart.

"OK, you're right," he said, his perfectly formed lips moving away from hers. "Come, Les Invalides."

Determinedly, they walked down the street until they found a *tête de station* to wait for a taxi.

The streets were silent now as they drove toward

the former barracks. Again, Marcy tucked her arm within his when they alighted from the taxi and strolled along the Esplanade and across the expanses of lawn, no longer the bright summer green Marcy had somehow expected from all the photos of Paris she had seen.

"Look at the moat. Was it once filled?" she murmured, gazing at the wide gully and the ramparts lined by cannons.

"Probably," Yves muttered. But it was clear he was not interested. Suddenly, he stopped and turned toward her again. "I think I would prefer to do this." He turned and clutched her to him.

Quickly, he slid his fingers into the buttons of her coat and undid them, as if he'd watched them all evening and knew exactly how to unfasten them. He peeled it open. His hands groped for her body, firmly caressing her. Again, her heart knocked as she felt his urgency grow.

"Oh, golly," she breathed, straining to catch her breath. Far off, she heard cars rolling over the pavement and a horn's insistent sound. She clung to him, madly returning the kisses he planted on her face as his hands ran down her thighs and roughly pulled up her skirt. Their bodies writhed against each other in the cool Paris night.

Here? She wanted to say. Why not? She didn't care. She craved an end to the dizzy hunger. She heard him unzip his pants and felt him juggle his body, to remove his member from within. Marcy stepped back against the gate, to have something to lean against.

She saw her breath congeal in the cold air and pressed her lips against his chest. Her legs were wet with desire. His hand reached under her sweater and shirt and covered her breasts in their little black lace home.

Then, he plunged himself against her forcefully, not yet entering her. She responded as they placed their bottom parts against each other in rhythmic beating. The tingling swarmed through her limbs til they ached for release. She pressed harder, silently pleading with this body to enter her.

Abruptly, he lurged against her so powerfully and grabbed her shoulders so forcefully that she knew it was over. Just like Kurt.

But with Kurt, she had been sad, bewildered, sympathetic. Not angry, as she was now.

"What about me?" she wailed looking up, tears filling her eyes.

"I'm sorry, I'm sorry. You were so delicious. I didn't have time. I will do it for you, if you like."

Repugnance swelled through her as she looked at his fluid massed on her black lace panties. What was she left with? This gop and—nothing. She shook her head angrily. The heat had suddenly dissipated.

"Take me home."

Silently, she sat in the taxi with him. Was she angry because he had dirtied her? Or frustrated her? It was the latter. She didn't ever care about that other stuff, but now he left her as driven as ever. Marcy took a deep, quavering breath, trying to control herself.

"I'm sorry," he repeated.

"It's OK. I guess. She smiled ruefully and picked up his hand. "I felt gypped."

"Gypped? I don't understand."

"I just didn't get what I was hoping for." She smiled sadly.

"I'm sorry about that too. Do you want to send me the cleaning bill?" He nodded toward her lap.

He seemed so penitent that she shook her head, and looked at him kindly. "You're forgiven, but only if you call me again."

Yves smiled delightedly, and gave her his arm as they walked up the steps to the mansion. "I will. I promise." He kissed her quickly on each cheek.

Marcy stood before the bathroom sink holding the panties, thick with his fluid, in her hand, about to wash it. Gingerly, she placed her forefinger on the spot and then brought it to her lips. It tasted salty, yet sweet, yet tasteless. She placed her finger on it again and touch it into her mouth again. Yes, this was new to her, and not unpleasant either.

She smiled. Well, at least something good had come out of tonight. But you sure can't count on an 18-year-old. "I guess I was right," she mused. "They probably are too young for me." An uneasy feeling nagged at her. What about Kurt at just 18? Why should he be any better? Had Mr. Van Couvering aged her too quickly, made her unsuitable for anything attainable?

She hung the panties to dry, and inspected the rest of her clothes to insure they weren't covered with the remnants of Yves' lust. That's a boy for you. Mr. Van Couvering would never do that. A sudden smile broke out. "What if I told Giselle? She'd tease her brother til the cows came home."

Marcy prepared for bed and then, pulling on her flannel nightie, ready for another night of secret passion, slipped between the cold cotton sheets.

This time, she thought, she must make her finger work like a man. But it was in vain. The finger just would not do. She tossed and turned, unsatisfied. What was she to do? How could she bear this?

She heard footsteps and mumbling. Was it he? Then more footsteps and silence. Utter silence. So, she thought ruefully, he would not be coming, after all. We've been away from each other so long, he'd forgotten about his nightly trysts.

She flipped on the bed light and sat up. She'd write Kurt. That would quell things. For when she wrote him, she became another person. She became the person she was when she left: ignorant, innocent, a babe in the woods. Not a woman who had had men and other women. But, oh, she yearned for release, and writhed desperately in her bed, her fingers trying to emulate her employer's.

She started at a tap at the door. Gleefully,

already knowing, she bolted upright and ran to it. There, before her stood Mr. and Mrs. Van Couvering. What could they want? Both of them? It wouldn't matter. Anything, just anything, to release her. Marcy smiled broadly.

"Come, Marcy," Mrs. Van Couvering took her hand. "We want you with us. We'd like to welcome you to France."

Marcy nodded in understanding. Mrs. Van Couvering stood before her in a pale pink satin robe, Mr. Van Couvering in a maroon cashmere robe, his initials on the breast pocket. Mrs. Van Couvering moved, leading Marcy down the wide hallway with the dimly lit sconces.

Side by side, the three then walked down the immense halls to the far bedroom. As the door shut behind them, Marcy stared in wonderment at the enormous bed with its giant four posters before her. Surely, it was big enough for the three of them.

But those were not the plans.

"Marcy," said Mr. Van Couvering, as he sat on the side of the bed. "Please. Watch us. We want you to watch."

"Why?" She stammered, uncomprehending. "Am I doing something wrong? All you need to do is tell me, or show me." She beseeched him.

"No," he chortled. "Nothing wrong, whatsoever. But this will give Mrs. Van Couvering and myself some pleasure, having you watch." He inclined his head toward an armchair placed at the foot of the bed. "Please, be comfortable."

His tone was so authoritative that Marcy timidly perched on the front of the chair and regarded Mr. Van Couvering. He undressed himself, carefully folding his robe over the back of the straight pull-up chair next to him. Then he leaned over and disrobed Mrs. Van Couvering who stood next to him. Her perky breasts gleamed in the soft light of the porcelain lamp on one side of the bed.

Marcy's throat tightened as that unquenched gnawing flooded her limbs yet again. Helplessly, she watched Mr. Van Couvering pull his wife toward him, bend over and place his mouth on her small breasts. Nimbly, he kissed them, while one hand groped for her buttocks and the other ran over the curves of her perfect, little body.

"Ohh," Mrs. Van Couvering moaned.

Or was it Marcy? For Marcy didn't know. All she knew was that her suffering was insurmountable. She placed her foot beneath her, to rock herself into release. Sweat broke out on her forehead as the fiery pit inside her grew hotter. She bit her lower lip till blood spurted. But still, she could not dampen her lust. Transfixed, she looked at Mr. Van Couvering carry his wife to the bed and insert his fingers into her and listened as she — or perhaps herself — moaned with infinite pleasure — or perhaps frustration.

Mrs. Van Couvering's fingers pressed into Mr. Van Couvering's bottom hole splaying the two halves apart. His legs tightened and his toes dug into the bed covers beneath. Marcy heard him groan and saw him arch.

She pressed her foot harder against her private parts and rocked furiously. Shocks of more heat tore through her—but no more. That release, the exquisite appreciation, was not to be hers. Panting sorrowfully, she looked on, unable to remove her eyes from the two people pressing urgently against each other.

Was it always to be thus tonight? Only watching? Helping others to come to their contentment? Marcy moaned in desperation.

Mrs. Van Couvering rolled on top of her husband and then settled herself on top of his standing member. Together they grunted. Marcy watched his toes curl and his behind tighten.

Without thinking, she stood and walked over to the bed. Still, without thinking, feeling only that she must end her suffering, she slid onto the bed, drew up her nightgown and slid next to Mrs. Van Couvering.

Mrs. Van Couvering smiled at her and moved her fingers toward Marcy's lower parts. There, she expertly fingered the girl, drawing her to the desired climax. Marcy grabbed Mr. Van Couvering's thigh in her hands feeling the hair against her palm, feeling him tense under her touch. The three grunted together, and moved rapidly together, with a frantic rhythm of the possessed. And then, as if in concert, the three of them came in unison.

"Ohhh,ohh." Marcy fell across Mrs. Van Couvering's back, as she moved forward onto her husband's chest. The three lay, thus entwined for many moments, feeling their mutual exhaustion and exhilaration.

At last, Marcy sat up. "I think I intruded. I overstepped my bounds. I'm sorry." But really, she was giddy with joy. Finally, she had come.

"Not at all. This was an unexpected pleasure," said Mr. Van Couvering sitting up and running his fingers through his wife's hair as he often did to Marcy's.

Mrs. Van Couvering rolled off her husband and nodded in agreement. "And did you have a nice evening, Marcy, with Yves?"

Marcy smiled. Mrs. Van Couvering was such a lady, always so solicitous of her. "Very nice, thank you. We walked around Montparnasse." Again thanking them, she bid the Van Couverings good-night.

Back in her room, Marcy sighed contentedly, as she lay back among the pillows. It was almost 3:00 A.M., but she didn't care to sleep yet. She finally had that release she'd been yearning for since Mr. Van Couvering had left for France.

But, still, she was nagged by the same thought. Who was she now? Was she anyone her parents and Kurt would want to reclaim? Yes, she still wore her High Flats skirts and blouses and shoes, but underneath them, who was she? Could she change back for them, and did she want to change? Yes, she still wanted the babies and Kurt, so in that way she hadn't changed. But had these newfound desires altered her so that Kurt would not want her any longer?

Troubled, she hastily wrote him about her day, turned off the light and went to sleep.

# CHAPTER 5

Marcy and Alexandra were to spend the days in luxurious freedom, with a young secretary, Monique, from Daniel's office as guide and translator. Monique was dutiful and nice, though not the sort of fun Parisian Marcy had come to expect from Giselle or Yves. She was quite short, somewhat overweight, with too-blonde hair and thick black mascara encasing her eyes. Still, she knew where to take them, how to get them there, and how to be companionable.

By metro, Monique led them to the Eiffel Tower. Marcy, never before on any underground transportation, gazed at every passing rider, at the charming doors that opened and closed almost soundlessly, at the little ticket stubs she received, and at the maps that lit up when she pressed a button for her destination.

"Come, we'll go up," Monique said, heading toward the lift that would take them effortlessly to the 1,000-foot peak. "We'll go to the top." The three each handed 40 francs to the tolltaker so they could see Paris from the third level.

Marcy stared in wonder. For the day, a bold winter's day, was crystalline. She saw the 42 miles of city and suburb that Monique had promised.

She held Alexandra in her arms so she also could peer out.

"This looks like the map of Paris that my ninth grade French teacher handed out, that we had to color in and memorize," she giggled, looking at well-known, but forgotten to her, buildings and boulevards. "Oh, I think I see the Louvre, and the Champs Elysées. And the Arc de Triomphe," she bubbled, caught in the excitment. "And the Left Bank and—" she stopped. "It's all so exciting," she said, catching herself. "I'm just so lucky to be here."

"I know when I come to the U.S.," Monique answered, pushing back her hair, "I will want to see everything." Her eyes, in thick black mascara, crinkled when she smiled. "I am sorry it's winter, or we could go to an amusement park in the Bois de Boulogne or the wonderful Bois de Vincennes for the gardens and flowers."

"You've been wonderful even in winter," Marcy countered, patting Monique's elbow.

"But, I have an idea. Let us go to the Place de la Madeleine, see a beautiful church, walk down the Rue du Faubourge St.-Honore, and have delicious pastries." She smiled at Alexandra. "I will give you a very French lunch of cheese and butter on long bread called *baguettes*."

Monique then turned to Marcy. "This afternoon, after her nap, I have a child for her to play with, who speaks English, because her father is American."

Thus, they whiled away that day and the days after that, sometimes playing with a neighboring child, or baking cookies and molding silly clay animals. Sometimes they would stroll down the Rue de Rivoli and quays next to the Seine, Alexandra running ahead, Marcy gazing in delight at the sights unfolded before her.

Or while Alexandra napped, Marcy would comfortably take herself, or have Daniel invite her, to a museum. At the Louvre she would stand before the paintings she'd long heard of: da Vinci's Mona Lisa, Murillo's Young Beggar, Tintoretto's Suzanna Bathing. She'd admire the triptychs, the Boulle Cabinets and the "Loves of the Gods" tapestries, or just wander, amassing the feel of the great space until closing.

At the Pompidou, with its steel and glass walls, pipes and conduits, Marcy would always stare at the structure, trying to determine why it was so loved, before wandering through the modern art exhibits.

At the Jeu de Paume, she wandered among her beloved impressionists: Degas, Monet and Sisley, as well as Cezanne and Renoir and others that she'd only known from text books.

The days, of course, were most fun with Daniel. Of course she was entranced by his charm and sophistication and fine sense of humor that easily had her laughing. But, more than that, she had a similar outlook. They shared values of family and work ethics, of loyalty and friendship. She found herself thinking more and more of Daniel, but he was polite and distant, the epitome of propriety, touching only her elbow in an occasional attempt to guide her someplace.

Though Marcy spent her days and the early part of the nights with others, the late parts belonged to the Van Couverings'.

For she spent them with her master and mistress. Late, upon their return, there would be a tap at the door. They would stand before her, dressed for bed. Unspeaking, she would follow them down the long corridor to the silence of their large heavily draped room.

And they would be together. Sometimes Mr. and Mrs. Van Couvering, while Marcy would watch. Sometimes Mr. Van Couvering and Marcy. or Marcy and the wife. Several times, at Mrs. Van Couvering's behest, they watched each other engage themselves alone. And, naturally, the three of them would also fall upon each other.

The days passed into each other, and Marcy, knowing she would usually have an evening's pleasure before her, rarely thought about seeing other men — or women. She was content with her life, and only feared it would not last.

For after the New Year, she and Alexandra would return to the States, and she did not know if the Van Couverings would come also, or when. If they stayed on in Europe, then with whom would she attend to her needs? For although Giselle and Sigrid had introduced her to men, there'd been none she was the slightest bit interested in. Ah, well, she might have to make do with someone from the University after all. Perhaps they had found someone else for her in her absence.

But, now, Marcy put these thoughts from her mind. For tonight was Christmas Eve. She and Alexandra had dressed the tree earlier in the day, hung strands of cranberries and glass globes of untold beauty on the fragile arms of the tree. And then she and the Van Couverings had stood around the tree and sung carols.

Directly before bed, Alexandra scampered into the kitchen for bisquits and milk to place on the mantel for Santa. Contentedly, she then walked up the wide staircase with her mother.

Marcy grinned at Mr. Van Couvering. "Now, sir, you must eat Santa's snack, or she will know there is no Santa."

He walked toward the mantel and lifted the glass. "And what would you like from Santa?"

"Nothing special. I'm happy. Just being here is enough." Marcy toyed with a delicate enamel egg laying on its end. "We never had much from Santa when I was little. There were five girls and not much money."

"Well," said Mr. Van Couvering, as he put the two bisquits at once into his mouth. "I'll see that he does better by you this year." He glanced at his watch. "We're late, I'm afraid. We ought to be back shortly after midnight. And you?"

"Yves, sir."

"Have a very nice time." He strode out of the room.

Marcy looked after him, wondering if he knew of her one experience with Yves, wondering what he knew about her at all. Marcy knew that Mr. Van Couvering was aware that she'd never had much contact with Kurt, but would he be angry about Yves? Did he feel that she ought to belong to the Van Couverings alone?

She hoped not. For she knew that he liked being her teacher. Somehow, though, as varied and as satisfying as her times with Mr. and Mrs. Van Couvering had been, they seemed limited. They all knew each other so well now, that the mystery was gone. If she were to settle with Kurt — and every day the time grew shorter and her questions grew longer — she would have to experience new things more quickly. Besides, a few more experiences could not possibly make her parents and Kurt reject her any more than they might already.

Once she had crossed the line of unbridled passion, she had dared them anyway. What was a little more?

Now, Marcy dressed for her second date with Yves, handsome Yves. If only he could perform with the grace his body promised. They had seen each other several times since that first night, but never alone.

She sensed his embarrassment, which he attempted to conceal by planting them among

74

many people. He'd entertain her well: walking in Montparnasse, Les Halles, the Champs Elysées, to nightclubs, cafes, parties where his friends would kindly speak English. Where he'd failed in one endeavor, he'd taught in another.

"*Bon jour,* Yves," Marcy smiled at him and held out her hand.

Again, as usual, he took it and placed it to his lips. She shivered. She wished he would do more, but it was clear he wanted to stay away, in case he failed again.

"I heard from my sister. She is missing you and hopes you will return soon."

Marcy nodded, somewhat torn. "Next week. I miss her, too, but I love it here. *C'est la vie.*" She shrugged. "What can I do? When my employer leaves, I leave. Well, anyway, what are we doing tonight?"

"I thought I would bring you to my parents.' To see our tree."

Marcy's heart sank. What a Christmas celebration. She thought she'd be at a party. Instead, she'd spend the evening with his parents.

"This is usually a family night. People stay with relatives, and go to church at midnight. My parents are with some relations now, so you will not meet them." He smiled. "The house is set up for Christmas Eve anyhow, and it is pretty."

Marcy nodded not feeling reassured. Reluctantly, she climbed into the taxi, heading for his apartment.

It was warm, friendly. Christmas cards, hanging from broad red ribbons, festooned the front hall and living room walls. The Christmas tree spread its magnificent branches over the room. A fire burned, the flames cavorting eagerly with one another.

"Some wine?" Yves asked, as she settled into the beige silk couch.

"No, thank you. Just a soda or something." Marcy slipped her feet out of her pumps and placed them under her, hugging her knees to her chest. She knew her thighs showed provocatively. She stared at the fire, wishing for something different.

Yves returned and glanced at her legs. He sat next to her, holding a Coca Cola and a Perrier and two wine glasses.

"I wanted to talk to you, Mar-cie," he began hesitantly, placing everything on the table. "About that night. I want to apologize. It was—how you say—immature. It had not happened to me before, and I don't know why it happened then. Perhaps you seem more experienced than the other women I have known."

"Shh," Marcy placed her finger to his lips, touched by his concern. "Don't say anything else. You have been a wonderful friend to me here. And I would not have had such a great time without you." She leaned forward and firmly kissed his lips. He returned the kiss, his tongue just touching hers.

Surprised, because he had not touched her since that night, Marcy let their tongues play together languidly. Then, she felt a light hand on her breast. Encircling it, his hand lifted it up further in its brassiere. The other hand discreetly unbuttoned her cotton blouse until she was exposed: her voluptuous breasts in the skimpy black bra.

"Oo-la-la," he whispered. "Beautiful." Yves slid his hand into the cup and merely lifted out a breast. He did the same with the other. Not taking his eyes off them, as they hung like full balloons, he reached behind to unsnap her bra. It fell to Marcy's elbows.

But she remained motionless, waiting to see what the Frenchman would do. How a young man, and a French man, would differ. He reached under her full skirt and unsnapped the black stockings from their garters, a recent Parisian acquisition to substitute for pantyhose. He pulled them to her ankles. Then, brusquely, he raised her skirt to her waist and buried his face in her mound, lying peacefully within her panties.

Marcy wriggled as the familiar wetness seeped into her lower parts. Her nipples were taut with expectation.

"Ahh, too good," he murmured. "Again, the problem."

"Just wait a moment. Hush," Marcy responded, halfway thinking that he was not the Frenchman she had imagined in her dreams. "Stop, til you get control."

They lay back, Marcy upon his covered chest. Slowly she unbuttoned his white shirt, revealing smooth, strong skin. Then she reached for his pants and, opening it quickly, stared at Yves' restrained member within his underwear. She toyed with the tuft of hair beneath his navel. Then, suddenly curious, she pulled his underwear away, and gasped at the enormity of his member. It stood upright, longer than anything she could possibly have imagined.

And, quickly, desiring nothing more, she bent over it, placing her full lips on the shaft. She ran her tongue over it, listening to him moan, feeling his thighs clench as her breasts balanced on them. He gripped her behind and ran his fingers over her firm stomach.

Teasingly, Marcy flicked her tongue over the end of his member, and pulled at it playfully with her lips.

"Oh, please, Mar-cie," he muttered. "Please. Stop. I won't be able to control myself."

But she did not. She cradled his testicles. For she knew what she wanted. She knew what he could teach her that she had not yet been taught. So she did not relinquish her hold with her gentle lips. She pushed her mouth far upon his sword. And then, like a flash, she felt the liquid spurt into her mouth, cover her lips, seep down her chin. Gamely, she swallowed, but it seemed as if his hotness would never end.

Without removing her lips from the still-hard

member, Marcy looked up. His eyes were closed. A smile crossed his face. His hands rested lightly on her.

"Yves," she whispered. "Thank you. That was your gift to me." She kissed the tip and drew back.

"Thank you? I failed you. Again," he sighed, righting himself.

"No," she grinned. "Not that time. That was something I wanted." Marcy sat upright, placing her breasts back in her bra, buttoning her blouse, and smoothing her skirt.

"But what can I do for you?" he asked, rather mournfully.

"You did it. Not a thing." She smiled complacently. "Now, let's have those drinks."

For what Marcy knew, and Yves did not, was that Mr. and Mrs. Van Couvering would soon be home.

# CHAPTER 6

"Get up, Marcy," a tiny hand shook Marcy's arm. "Come on."

"What time is it?" Marcy turned toward the clock on the night table. "It's 6:00, Alexandra," she groaned.

"But it's Christmas!"

"I forgot!" Marcy bounded out of bed, remembering her own Christmases when she was a child. "You're right. Go wake mommy and daddy."

"I already did. They're putting on their robes." Alexandra clapped her hands excitedly.

"Let me wash up." Marcy felt her way into the marble bathroom to splash water on her face, trying to arouse herself still further. The Van Couverings must feel as fatigued as she, since it was well after midnight when the three retired.

Marcy buttoned her wool robe, slipped her feet into her snug slippers and followed the girl. Mr. and Mrs. Van Couvering were standing at the head of the staircase waiting for them.

"We thought you'd never get up," teased Mr. Van Couvering, his dark hair still tousled from sleeping.

"Almost couldn't. Not til I remembered the day," returned Marcy, grabbing the bannister.

"Let's go," Alexandra demanded, taking her mother's hand down the wide staircase.

At the bottom stood the magnificent 10-foot tree, brightly lit, awash with glittering ornaments. Underneath lay mountains of Christmas gifts.

Marcy, like Alexandra, stared in astonishment. Never had she seen such a mass of gifts. In High Flats, these many gifts could have been split among all her sisters, her parents, grandparents and aunts and uncles. "Are these all for—us?"

"Of course not," laughed Mrs. Van Couvering, "but we like to pile everything under the tree for everybody."

"Ah," Marcy breathed a sigh of some relief. But, still, even knowing that, Alexandra seemed to have endless gifts to unwrap from cousins, aunts, uncles, family friends and her parents.

The black-garbed maid brought in coffee for Mr. and Mrs. Van Couvering and orange juice for Marcy and Alexandra as the three stood around watching the little girl unwrap a rocking horse and a bicycle, a talking doll, a little watch, a talking television. Then, finally, Alexandra stopped. Plaintively, she looked at Marcy. "Did you give me anything?"

Marcy nodded and waded among the ripped wrapping paper to the giant mahogany door where she had dropped her gift in its dazzling silver wrapping. She held it out.

"Gosh, Marcy, oh, thank you. I love it. I will love it forever!" She held aloft a soft, black velvet

81

dog. A heart was embroidered on its chest with the letters A and M.

"I made it myself," Marcy beamed, unable to contain her pleasure.

"Then I love it even more."

Marcy felt Mr. and Mrs. Van Couvering's admiring glances on her beautifully embroidered animal.

"When did you have time?" Mrs. Van Couvering asked, folding her arms across the now familiar satin robe.

"At night. After Alexandra went to bed," she replied. Before you would come for me, she said to herself, I would sew, half-concentrating on my little stitches, and half-concentrating on the footsteps to come.

But now, Marcy turned her attention back to the matter at hand. Happily, she watched Mrs. Van Couvering unwrap emerald and diamond earrings and necklace from her husband, and the painting of the flower from her daughter. She saw Mr. Van Couvering open his cashmere sports jacket with antique gold buttons and his ash tray made of yellow Playdough from Alexandra.

"Now, you, Marcy," he said.

"Me?" For who would give her gifts beside Alexandra? Her mother had sent her a red cardigan sweater which she'd opened in Delaware, and Kurt had sent a pear-shaped silver pin. But surely not Mr. and Mrs. Van Couvering. She had bought them nothing. Hesitantly, she bent over and picked up a large box with her name on it from Lanvin.

As the folds of tissue paper swirled to the ground, Marcy lifted two silk shirts, one in white, the other beige.

"Ohh," she gasped joyously, fingering their softness that felt like melted butter to her fingers. "They are absolutely beautiful."

In the other Lanvin box were a pair of black wool high-waisted pants, cut full on her legs, and a tight black skirt. She knew, as she held the skirt up that, unlike her present skirts, it would scarcely brush the tops of her knees. She blushed at the prospect.

"Here." Alexandra held out a small box. "From me."

Marcy slowly took off the white cardboard box cover and pulled out a gold locket and long thin chain. She snapped the locket open. There, smiling, was a photo of the little girl. Tears filled her eyes and she bent toward her, pulling her closer. She kissed Alexandra's cheek.

"Thank you. My best present ever," Marcy reached the two ends of the chain behind her neck to clasp them together. The locket fell between the cleft of her breasts.

Silently, she looked at Mrs. Van Couvering to thank her for having participated in the gift.

"And now," said Mrs. Van Couvering briskly, "let's have some breakfast," for the smell of bacon and eggs and croissants wafted into the living room. "We'll play with our new things later," she said, looking fondly at Alexandra, "and then pack for the Bergeracs."

Marcy shook her head agreeably. They were off to the Van Couverings' friends for two nights. Tomorrow would be a lavish party. She wondered what would become of her. She supposed she'd stay upstairs as the proper *au pair* once Alexandra's presence was no longer required. For, clearly, these two days were beyond anything someone like her could be expected to participate in comfortably. Anyway, she shrugged to herself, she had nothing to wear.

But it was when she returned to her room after a festive breakfast that she changed her mind.

There, swatched in tissues, laying on her bed, was a long black crepe gown. For her, she knew, also from Mr. and Mrs. Van Couvering. It was their way of telling her she was expected at the festivities also. Quickly, Marcy slipped out of her robe and nightgown and pulled the dress over her head. It was virtually strapless except for two inch-wide straps that attached to the bodice of the long tight dress.

Gaping, she stood before the mirror, transformed. Her breasts were framed within the crepe material like perfect melons. Her fine waist was accented by the pleats at her hips. Her legs were enveloped by a clinging skirt.

"Oh, golly," she breathed rapturously.

"May I come in?" Mrs. Van Couvering opened

the door and stood before her.

"I can't believe this is me," Marcy exploded when she saw Mrs. Van Couvering. "Thank you, a million."

"Lovely, just perfect." Mrs. Van Couvering nodded, her eye missing nothing. "Try this." She held out a jeweled hair clip. "Put your hair up."

Marcy did as she was told and stared in disbelief. She was no longer a schoolgirl, but finally, in looks, a woman. For months she'd felt like a woman, but now the transformation was complete. A woman stood before this mirror in Paris. A voluptuous, gorgeous woman.

"Thank you ever so much. I—I don't know how to thank you."

"Marcy, you've been a treasure. Think nothing of this."

Spontaneously, Marcy leaned over and kissed Mrs. Van Couvering's cheek. Mrs. Van Couvering held her a moment longer than necessary and then released the younger woman, though her fingers lingered on Marcy's supple waist.

"Lemme take this off so I don't crush it." Marcy eased the dress over her head and carefully hung it on one of the plush satin hangers in the cedar closet. She felt her mistress' eye roaming over her naked body and flushed with embarrassment. But Mrs. Van Couvering only looked approvingly.

"You'll join us at all occasions at the Bergeracs, please, Marcy. Once Alexandra is in bed, you'll be free as usual."

Marcy nodded and leaned over to pick up her nightgown from the bed.

"Here, let me." Mrs. Van Couvering's hands reached up and slipped the red flannel nightgown over Marcy's head and sensuously smoothed it over her breasts, waist and hips. There her fingers stayed, then returned to Marcy's breasts. Slowly, she rotated her palms against them til Marcy found her nipples grow taut and moisture damping her crotch.

"Oh, Mrs. Van Couvering," she whispered, her breath beginning to come harder. "Do you think this is the time?"

For an answer, the woman led Marcy into the bathroom, turned on the shower, slipped out of her clothes and removed Marcy's. They entered the shower together. Mrs. Van Couvering ran the bar of soap over Marcy's body til a fine lather covered her. She paused at Marcy's inner thighs, lightly massaging the soap around Marcy's tender parts. Marcy began to wriggle, as Mrs. Van Couvering revolved the bar of soap around Marcy's vulva. Marcy reached out and pulled Mrs. Van Couvering to her, bent over to kiss her fine breasts, and then insert her own fingers into the other woman. Standing under the sparkling drops, the women writhed and touched one another until their lust was satisfied.

Marcy stuck out her tongue, lapping up the water. "I loved that," she giggled, pushing her hair behind her ears.

"I love anything in the water," Mrs. Van Couvering replied. "How about you?"

"My first time." To herself, she added, everything I do is practically my first time.

The two stepped out of the shower, dressed and attended to their packing.

The chateau rose in the distance, southwest of Paris, beyond St. Cloud, beyond Versailles, nestled within rolling hills. Marcy could only imagine their lustre in spring. Like a fortress, the chateau seemed to command everything around it.

The chauffeured car drove up a long, wide tree-lined boulevard to a circular drive and the mammouth building that would house Marcy for two nights. A fountain, silent in winter, commanded the center of the drive.

To the right she spied horse stables, located near barren woods. In the distance, beyond the stables were tennis courts. Under the light covering of snow, she noted pristine paths leading to even more pristine gardens. It seemed like a never-ending fairy tale.

"This is wonderful," she murmured as she was introduced to her host, M. Bergerac, a handsome man of 30, master of this magnificence.

"Thank you. I'm pleased to meet you. M. Van Couvering has spoken so well of you."

Marcy froze.

"You have been remarkable for Alexandra," he continued, clearly not understanding the cause of her fright. "I wish we could find someone half so engaging for our son, Jacques, whom you will meet."

"Thank you, monsieur. I look forward to meeting him."

M. Bergerac led Marcy to his wife and several other older guests. She felt out of place and searched in vain for her employers. But there was no familiar face there. And these guests, while cordial, clearly wished to talk intimately, in French, among themselves.

"If you'll excuse me," she managed, stepping back to the entrance of the room. Nervously, she twisted her fingers among each other and looked at the guilded lamps resting on angels on either side of the piano. Where were Mr. and Mrs. Van Couvering? Where was Alexandra? Panic rose.

"At least *we* will know each other," a vaguely familiar voice, not the one she expected, spoke into her ear.

Marcy wheeled around to face Daniel. "Oh, and thank goodness. I was feeling so lost and awkward and not knowing what to do with my gawky self." With relief, Marcy flipped her hair behind her ears.

"I, too, could use a friend," he rejoined. "It is my great pleasure to be your escort." Daniel took her elbow and turned her attention to the front hall.

Marcy gazed at his sandy brown hair, gracefully curling over the tops of his ears. She admired his powerful, stocky build. He was built like Kurt, though shorter.

"You don't know anyone either?" she ventured, eyeing a black Mercedes that had just driven up.

"Not many. So I think we should escape here for awhile. I just passed M. and Mme. Van Couvering who said they will spend the next few hours with Alexandra and the Bergeracs' son. Will you be kind enough to join me? Have you any boots?"

"Yup," she smiled gratefully. He was like a Greek god, coming to rescue her. And they were even in the same boat of not knowing anyone. "They're upstairs. Someone brought my suitcase upstairs. But I haven't been upstairs yet. I don't even know which way to go." Marcy whirled her head from side to side.

"Let me escort you there. I'll find out what wing you're in."

In a moment he returned, talking amiably with another man. "The North Wing. Your room is next to Alexandra's and down the hall from the Van Couverings." He nodded to two women passing by, took the hand for a quick kiss of a third.

As they ambled down the wide hallway, he stopped momentarily to chat familiarly with two men passing by in high boots and winter coats, on their way out. Another clapped him on the back. Still another pumped his hand in greeting.

Marcy watched in amusement, a sudden suspicion growing that he indeed was not friendless here, but that he had pretended to be, to make her feel more comfortable. Her heart warmed at the thought of his kindness toward her.

Daniel led her down giant halls and staircases until, finally, he stopped before a door. "This is the Green Room."

"You know it so well. Have you been here before?"

"Occasionally. Fox hunting, polo, fishing. Various times of the year over various years."

"You do know a lot of people," Marcy said. "You were just teasing." She opened the door, still looking at him.

"Indeed. Most of us have gone to school together in some fashion, or done business, or have had relatives who have done business with one another over the years." He stopped. "But there is no one I prefer to be with more than you."

"Oh," Marcy breathed as she stopped in the doorway to admire the Green Room. Great swaths of pale green draperies hung from enormous windows. French country bureaus, desk and bed lined the room.

"This is like the Louvre," she said simply, running her hand along the wooden desk.

"Except it doesn't have that modern I.M. Pei lobby," Daniel responded smiling.

"You're right. How many other rooms do they have?" Just wait'll she wrote her mother. It made the Delaware mansion pale in comparison.

"About 120 altogether."

"Is the rainbow that big to give all the rooms

different color names?"

"No, madamoiselle," he laughed. "Some have names like the Library and the Great Room and the Small Room. But the bedrooms, they have names of color."

Marcy twirled around, imagining her whole house fitting into just three colorful rooms. "But where are my clothes?" For, nowhere could she see her suitcase.

Daniel flung open a large armoire and pointed. *"Ici."*

Someone had already unpacked her few belongings and hung her pants and crepe dress and silk blouse in the armoire. There, in the corner, as if in hiding, were the leather and rubber lace-up winter boots she'd brought east from High Flats. Certainly no match for the elegance she'd find today. She winced. She should have known enough to have replaced these boots days ago.

"Ah, a new fashion," Daniel said gamely, reaching for her boots. "I like these."

Marcy blushed, again appreciating his sensitivity toward her. She slipped into them, fetched her parka from the armoire and, together, headed through the woods and to the hills, with Daniel at her side.

They walked for several hours, for once not distracted by the horns of Paris, the gruff voices of the guards in the museums or brashness of shopkeepers. As they returned, Marcy's cheeks shone brightly like polished apples, her blue eyes radiated the sky's light.

She felt at ease with this man. He seemed to understand her background, what she hoped to gain from this year in the east, what she wanted when she returned to the midwest. He, too, spoke of himself. He grew up in a small town outside of Nice, went to the Wharton School of Finance and met M. Van Couvering. He hoped soon to settle down and have children.

Despite herself, Marcy found herself drawn to him in a way that she'd only been drawn to Kurt. His goals were her goals, his background was her background. They were so — *sympatico*. She struggled for the proper word, and amazed herself that it was French. Somehow, when she spoke to Daniel, this new world that she'd embarked upon six months ago did not seem so strange and intangible. She felt comfortably at ease with it.

As they approached the chateau, Daniel halted and turned toward her. Silently, he placed the tip of his finger under Marcy's chin, guiding it toward his own. Gently, he placed his lips upon hers. She returned the soft kiss and briefly closed her eyes in overwhelming happiness. For something told her that this was more than just a kiss of flesh upon flesh. This time with Daniel was meant to be.

He slipped his finger from her chin to her neck and then her arm. He took a step backward. Marcy did also. They looked at each other and smiled. A sudden calm engulfed her and she breathed deeply. No rush. She would rush nothing with him. There would be time, of that she was sure.

"We probably should be going back, Marcy," he mumbled. "To dress for dinner."

She nodded, mute.

"A small dinner at 8:00."

She would join them alone, for Alexandra would be asleep by then.

# CHAPTER 7

Content, as if floating on a luxurious cloud, she bounded up the staircase like a little girl to her room, threw her outer garments onto the bed and settled into the rose-colored silk wing chair with a pen and paper.

*"Dear Mom and Dad,"* she wrote, *"the chateau is fabulous. I know no one here except Mr. Van Couvering's assistant and he has shown me around. It is glamorous, like a palace. I wish I had a postcard to send you. It has over 100 rooms, though, of course, they don't keep the entire chateau open. I'll write later. I must put Alexandra to bed and dress for dinner."*

Marcy drew a line at the end of the section so her mother would know that when she next put pen to paper, time would have passed.

She waited in Alexandra's room until the Van Couverings returned her. The girl bubbled on about her day with Jacques as Marcy drew her bath, and wrapped her in pajamas. The day had been full. She and Jacques had ridden the pony in the indoor ring, had hitched him up to a cart, had skated on the pond. Tomorrow would be fuller, no doubt. Then, suddenly, in the middle of her sentence, Alexandra stopped, begged for sleep and

94

rolled over in the feather bed, engulfed in sleep.

Marcy leaned over to kiss her, and returned to her room. She dressed in the black skirt and white silk blouse that the Van Couverings had given her only that morning. They fit perfectly, as she knew they would. Mrs. Van Couvering knew her dimensions well. She examined herself in the mirror with pleasure and awe.

Her breasts stood firmly against the fabric, the tips appeared as playful little dots on the end. Her waist was cinched tightly, her legs long and lithe. The results were striking. If only Daniel would think so. For, until now, he had mostly seen her in a long navy wool coat she wore to walk the streets of Paris with him, and her skirt and sweater sets from High Flats.

Marcy pulled up her black stockings, fastened them to her black garter belt and slipped into her pumps. She grimaced again, for again she knew the footwear was wrong. But, she shrugged, too bad, she had no choice.

The dinner was intimate by chateau standards. Only 30 or so, at five different tables, elegantly laid with silver settings and spring flowers of anemones and fuchsia and lilacs. Daniel was her dinner partner.

She saw Mr. Van Couvering smile at her approvingly as she took her place. Had Mr. Van Couvering asked that Daniel be invited, or was it just a happy coincidence? No matter, she thought lightly. At least he was here.

As she raised her wine glass in a toast, she felt Daniel's thigh brush against hers. She drew her breath in sharply, as unexpected tingling surged through her loins. It frightened her. She eyed him shyly as he chatted in English to the elegant woman beside him.

She leaned toward M. Coulet, her partner to her left, relieved that she had managed to stanch the fire that seemed about the start. M. Coulet, the head of a glass manufacturing business, chatted about glass, as well as boating.

But all the time she spoke to him about his business and his boats, she knew she really wanted to be speaking with and touching the man on the other side of her. But she was terrified of his touch. And so, imperceptively, she leaned closer to M. Coulet.

After dinner the women retired to a living room, the men to the library. Marcy sat primly in one corner of a loveseat, listening to the French chatter that she could barely understand. From time to time, Mrs. Van Couvering would stop and smile at her, but then she, too, would return to foreign tongues.

Marcy itched to leave this group and join Daniel, but she knew that was improper. The men were to smoke and drink and talk business alone. Somehow, it didn't seem right to separate the two groups. Why, in fact, couldn't they speak together? Surely they had enough things in common. She snickered inwardly, imagining herself standing up to join the men in the other room. Her mother would sure take a dim view of that.

The women settled against the silken couches and armchairs, surrounded by lilies and irises, golden ashtrays and cloisonne boxes of different sizes. Portraits lined the walls, amid the heavy cinnamon-colored draperies.

At last, Marcy's mind drifting toward her companions' clothes, the men joined them. She gratefully smiled at Daniel when he sat next to her.

"Did you have a nice conversation?" she asked, folding her hands onto her lap.

"Very, thank you. And you?"

"In French," Marcy smiled ruefully. "But I got to look around a lot."

"At Mme. Penicaud? She's the wife of the largest auto dealer in France. And Mme. d'Effiat? The subject of a major scandal several years ago when she left her husband to marry M. d'Effiat. It was fortunate that she was the rich one."

"Go on," she urged, giggling.

"Ah, each one has a story. Here's another. Mlle. Perrault never showed up at the church on her wedding day 20 years ago, thinking at the last minute she could do better. But no one dared try her after that."

Marcy giggled again. "Really? Why didn't she move to another town?"

"She was too well known. Foolish. An expensive error in judgment."

Daniel lifted Marcy's pinky. "I trust you'll make

97

no such errors?"

She shook her head, and changed the subject. "How was your dinner?"

"Excellent. Although my dinner partner to my left chose to speak to the dinner partner on *her* left."

Marcy nodded, but said nothing. So he had noticed. Did he think she didn't like him? Or liked him too much?

"Why did you not speak to me during dinner, Marcy?" Daniel pressed, still holding her finger. "Were you angry about this afternoon? Did I say something wrong? Kiss you too soon?"

"Oh, no," she murmured softly, worried that she'd been misunderstood. "No, it was just that . . . that I thought it was rude to ignore the other man."

"I see." He hesitated. "Would you care to go out on the balcony?" Daniel stood, offering his hand which she accepted.

They walked through the French doors at the far end of the room to the balcony. Marcy shivered. Daniel placed his coat around her shoulders, letting his hands rest on them. He pulled her toward him and firmly placed his lips on hers.

She answered hungrily, opening her mouth as his tongue drove into her. He plunged deeply, exploring the recesses of her cheeks, pulling out quickly and reinserting it shallowly or deeply at will. Marcy breathed heavily, her heart hammering as he thrilled her entire body with just his tongue.

She craved to press her body against him and feel his strength next to her, but she knew that would be too forward. And inappropriate. Thirty guests were inside, lingering over cigars and coffee and brandy. Marcy pulled away, her chest heaving with desire.

"Not here," she whispered. An ache of desire lodged in her loins.

"No, of course not. How stupid of me." Silently, Daniel led her indoors, through the throng of guests who let them pass by unheeded, past the servants in the marble foyer, and up another staircase she'd not seen before.

"But mustn't we say goodnight to everyone?" Marcy asked softly.

"You say it to me, instead," he replied, his lips lightly caressing her neck.

He opened the massive wooden door to his large room. Heavy maroon draperies shielded the windows from the evening's cold darkness. A monstrously large, elaborately carved four-poster stood in the middle of the room, a king bidding them to come closer.

"Ah, Marcy," he breathed, turning on a shy light next to the bed. "I can scarcely wait."

Marcy nodded, trembling inwardly at the thought of his hands on her body, her thighs squeezed against his. She stood, her fingers clasped demurely in front of her, her strength ebbing.

Daniel leaned against one of the bed posts and appraised her body in her form-fitting clothes. Marcy shifted uneasily, wondering what was expected of her. What was she to do? Undress herself, undress him, undress each other?

But she needn't have worried. Daniel bent down and lifted one stockinged foot out of its pump and kissed the toes. Then the other. Still on his knees, he ran his fingers lightly up her calves, over her knees to her inner thighs. Marcy gasped as he neared her mound, but she didn't utter another sound. His fingers roamed sensuously over her legs, her buttocks and her hips, then down again.

Her breathing quickened as his fingers once again slipped under her skirt toward her upper thigh. She shivered in anticipation. This was so different from Mr. Van Couvering. This was so slow, so subtle, that it could, truly, proceed for hours. Vaguely, she recalled that Mr. Van Couvering always seemed so rushed, so business-like. But, this, this seemed to last forever.

Marcy licked her lips, her appetite whetted. She placed her hands on Daniel's thick hair and rubbed her fingers through it. She closed her eyes as she again felt his fingers patrol her legs and thighs. How hot would she become? Would he create in her a fiery pit she had never ever imagined?

Now, Daniel's hand rested lightly on her pubis. He gave a slight pressure, but nothing more. Marcy sighed and bent down to urge his hand against her more forcefully, as if asking him to unclothe her now. But he would not. His fingers lingered on her garments.

He stood and kissed her shoulder lightly, let his tongue parade over her neck and ears and lips and dart in and out of her mouth. Marcy reached out, hugging him to her. Without a thought, she began to unbutton his shirt. She pulled at his tie to free it, but it wouldn't budge. In fact, she mused, she'd never unfastened Mr. Van Couvering's. It had never seemed to matter. But tonight it did. She wanted to explore the mystery of this man's body more than she ever thought possible.

"Here, Marcy, let me," Daniel murmured, adroitly slipping it off. "Before you tear the silk."

Now his shirt fell open, revealing a smooth, muscular chest. Marcy rolled her fists against it, feeling its strength. She pulled the shirt off him and let it drop to the floor.

For the first time, Daniel placed his hands on her breasts, moving the flesh upwards and sideways. He toyed with her nipples through her clothing til they stood on end. She pushed against him, but he pulled back, so that only one of his finger tips touched her firm breasts, encircling the ends ever so lightly.

"Uh," Marcy gasped sharply as the turmoil welled within her.

She looked down to see his member pushing against his pants. Determined, she reached down and unbuttoned them easily til they slipped to the ground. Now Daniel stood before her virtually naked, his manhood swollen within the undershorts. She stepped forward, but he backed away.

"Ah, not yet, not yet. There will be time. Endless time. The first time is a wondrous time, so you must wait a bit," he whispered in her ear. His breath seared her flesh.

Marcy nodded, swallowing with difficulty. She knew she could last, but did she want to?

At last, he began to undo the buttons of her silk blouse. It fell carelessly to the floor. He buried his face into the full bosom that rose before him in their little white cups. Daniel's fingers slipped between the lace and the flesh, kneading her til she groaned with pleasure, a wild passion gripping her.

Again, Marcy reached for his member, now grown even larger within its fabric constraint. She rubbed it firmly with her fingers. With her other hand, she reached behind him to hold his flesh there, too. She felt him unclasp her bra and bend over her, covering her breasts with his mouth as if he would devour them.

Gently, he extricated her hold upon him and led her toward the massive bed. He placed her against the other post at the bed's foot so he could further undress her. Finally, her skirt and panties lay on the floor. She stood before him, clothed only in her black stockings and garter belt clinging to her slender hips.

He stepped out of his undershorts. Marcy's eyes roved over his strong, muscular, naked body and rested on his engorged manhood that seemed to throb with enthusiasm.

Daniels' gaze rested on her belly and the blonde pubis beneath. He turned her so she faced the bed, her hands resting on the mattress, her feet spread-eagle against the heavily designed maroon Persian carpet. His hands roamed over her body, lingering on her hips and buttocks, moving them in saucy circles. She heard him grunt his approval. Then she waited eagerly, as she felt him fumble for her opening and insert his massive member. He pushed against her slowly, as the waves of heat built. Then, as the passion grabbed hold, he held her and slammed inside her again and again until she shrieked with ecstacy.

When it was over, she fell forward, her arms spread out before her, her legs splayed apart. He lay on top of her, panting also. Marcy felt the sticky moisture between their bodies and her legs, and felt his now-softening member against her back thigh.

"That was nice," she panted into the heavy maroon velvet bed cover on which her head lay. It was wet where she had bitten it, grabbing it in her wild moments. The locket from Alexandra dangled between her breasts.

"Ah, *oui*," he rejoined.

Marcy said nothing more. She recognized only that this had been special, different from anything with Mr. Van Couvering or Yves. Those were delightful interludes, more physical, more in the nature of a game. But this, this held the sanctity of an emotional bond. He had begun to take that special place that Kurt had always held. And now she was afraid to break the spell.

"A shower?" he asked, slowly rolling off her and standing.

"Yup."

Marcy followed him into the shower. Now, looking at his soft member with regret, she wished they'd first done it in the water as she and Mrs. Van Couvering had only that morning. Oh, it all seemed so very long ago. "I love the water."

"We will make love here, too," Daniel beamed, kissing her cheek. Gently, he took the soap and lathered her back and buttocks, her breasts and stomach, the soft folds of her inner thighs.

She watched his broad, strong hand hold the soap and watched the muscles move in his forearm as he delicately swathed her body in the perfumed lather. Then, out of the corner of her eye, she watched his manhood begin to rise and harden firmly. She felt her own body begin to tingle with steamy hope.

Water streamed down their bodies. He lifted her, placed her mound hard on his manhood and rammed into her.

Marcy spent the next day apart as she cared for Alexandra. They ice skated and rode the pony and finger painted. She'd rather spend the day with the little girl than with the adult guests, for earlier she had seen Daniel and Mr. Van Couvering stroll down the lane, heads bent, clearly intent on business. Yes, she'd rather be with Alexandra than with those adults with whom, cordial as they were, she really did not belong.

Even if they did speak English in her presence, how could she join them in talks of charities, or clothes stores, upcoming theatre and dinner parties, trips to the Swiss and Austrian Alps for skiing or Barbados for sunning? Even the youngest women were still ten years older. And, even supposing there were other 18-year-olds, what would they have in common? She hadn't benefited from private schools and foreign travel, Louis XV furniture and Christolfe silverware.

Marcy knew she looked good in her silk blouse and wool pants from the Van Couverings, but she also knew that, despite the clothes, she was at a distinct distance behind all of them. At least with Alexandra, she was loved.

Eagerly, though, she awaited the evening ball. She couldn't wait to put on her dress and dance with Daniel. She craved his touch on her back and hips. She licked her lips with joy.

She had just zipped the back of the tight-fitting crepe dress when a light tap at her door startled her.

"Yes?" she called nervously, for who could it be?

"I wanted to see if you need any help," Mrs. Van Couvering strolled into the room, a vision in folds of white chiffon with a sequined short jacket. "Oh, Marcy, simply stunning."

"Not so stunning as you, Mrs. Van Couvering," Marcy retorted, gingerly touching the material before her.

"Here, let me put this clasp in your hair." Mrs. Van Couvering reached up and placed the clip in the golden tresses.

"Wonderful. An *au pair* to make us proud." Her eyes twinkled. "But we're not losing you, are we?"

"Oh no, of course not. I stay til June," Marcy protested. "If you want me too," she added hastily, suddenly afraid Mrs. Van Couvering had been hinting at something unpleasant.

"Not that way. Another way. You seem to have a beau." Mrs. Van Couvering smoothed the pleats at Marcy's hips.

"Oh, I see. No, no, I don't think so."

A fleeting, violent dream pricked her. If it were so obvious to Mrs. Van Couvering, then could Daniel see it also? Could there, in fact, be something strong and binding between them both? And yet, she knew she'd return to Paris tomorrow, and to Delaware several days after that. A pang darted through her.

"Well, enjoy yourself, now." Mrs. Van Couvering patted Marcy's shoulder. "I'll see you downstairs in a few minutes."

Marcy stared after her, wondering if she were miffed about Daniel's attentions. Did she think

Marcy would no longer lend her body to them in the nights? She grinned, for it seemed as if she had enough fire in her to go around for everyone — and still more. But enough of that. It was time to see Daniel. Eagerly, she descended the stairs to the ballroom.

She stopped stock-still in wonder at the entrance to the giant room. What had only yesterday been a massive empty room with mirrors lining either side and light blue draperies hanging from the 20-foot high windows with a sole piano at one end had been transformed into the Fairy Kingdom. Wooden nutcrackers, sugar plum fairies, glistening ballet slippers and gaily decorated packages dangled from the ceiling and the walls. A mammoth Christmas tree stood at attention in the middle of the room, around which dancers in black tuxedos and gloriously adorned dresses swirled.

Gay chatter on all sides, as guests congregated and congratulated Mme. Bergerac on her clever decorations, interrupted Marcy's reverie. She strained her neck upward, searching for Daniel amid the throngs.

"An escort?"

She wheeled around to find his easy smile at her side. *"Mais, oui,"* she smiled.

"You are a vision," he said, standing back to admire the long legs, slim hips and ample breasts gleaming above the tight black bodice. His hand pressed into her waist.

Marcy felt she could only endure the beautiful

evening. For sugarplum fairies were not what she wanted. What she wanted stood before her or next to her and sometimes behind her, dancing, conversing, laughing with her and with others.

What Marcy wanted was to be possessed by this man who had so captivated her that she could scarcely think of anything anymore. She longed for that omnivorous passion to grip them both again. Could he want that also, she wondered. She could not tell from his refined demeanor, carefully smiling and speaking with the other guests.

But, finally, they could leave. Daniel, too, lost not a moment in deftly sliding out the room and leading her to his quarters.

There, hour after hour, they engaged in endless torrents of ecstacy, ferocious grabbing and hurtling, til the wee hours of the morning came upon them. He took her standing with her legs gripped around him; with her on top, then him; sideways with their legs twisted around each other, naked and half-clothed. She'd stand in her black garter and black stockings, he'd stuff his manhood through the opening in his loose underwear; on the bed; legs flung over the arms of the wing chair; and on the floor. The maelstrom of desire swirled around them til Marcy lay fully spent on the Persian rug.

Then, sadly, as the first dawn broke, Marcy returned to her room, to shower and wash her hair. Today they would leave. It was over, yet how could it be? In these brief two days, Daniel had

become so important to her and she sensed she
had become so to him. Why couldn't they continue this in Paris? She still had almost a week, a
week to see if they needed more time together or
could make their critical choices now.

Kurt had fast faded into the background. As if
she'd never known him.

Could she stay on in Paris, she mused, pulling
up her stockings. Could she return to Paris in June
as his girlfriend and then his wife? Yes, it was true
they'd spent hours making love, but they had also
spent hours talking of feelings, family, hopes,
disappointments. She wanted him. She wanted his
sophistication and worldliness, his suavity and
kindness.

Kurt seemed so young, so innocent, something
she was not prepared to return to now. She shook
her head as she combed her long wet hair. How
disloyal. But wasn't that just the reason she came
east? To see what else there was? To grow? Yes.
But, in fact, she never expected to dump Kurt.
What on earth would her mother say about that?

Dully, Marcy packed her clothes in her black
vinyl suitcase and snapped it shut. Would she see
him in Paris? Would he call her nightly, so they
could spend the last few days together, planning?
When would he come to the United States? Could
she wait that long?

She pushed her vinyl suitcase by the door for the
servant to carry downstairs and place among the
Vuitton and Hermes bags. Then she joined the
Van Couverings' farewells.

# CHAPTER 8

Marcy awoke to a frosty Paris morning she intended to spend with Yves. Mr. and Mrs. Van Couvering had given her the remaining few days off, having made arrangements for Alexandra's care with some close friends with little children.

Marcy stretched, pulling herself up by the bedpost behind her. If only Daniel would call. They had returned to Paris together, he and she tightly squeezed together in the jump seat bench yesterday. The whole ride, whenever the car would bump, Marcy would catch her breath sharply at the pressure of his thigh jammed against hers. He had whispered that he'd call her.

Even when the phone rang for her last night and it was Yves, she nurtured the hope that Daniel would call and that she could cancel her plans with the other.

But he didn't call.

Quickly, Marcy showered and dressed herself in her beige silk blouse and wool pants with their full leg. She slid her feet into her trusty pumps. Ruefully, she smiled. She supposed she'd go to her deathbed with the wrong kind of footwear.

*"Mademoiselle?"* The maid inquired outside the door.

"*Oui?*" Marcy opened it to receive a letter. Perhaps Daniel. But it was from her mother. "*Merci.*"

Carelessly, she opened it. Always the same thing: news of the town sicknesses, school prizes, animal antics, announcements of weddings and funerals. She shrugged, then stiffened.

"*You're changed,*" her mother's letter reprimanded. "*What are you doing that is changing you? Is this how you want to change? Are you happy? Are you honest to me in your letters?*"

Marcy stopped, puzzled, trying to rethink the letters she'd sent home. She bit her lip, wishing she'd get copies of the first letters to compare to the current ones. Was it bad to change? Of course she should be expected to change from the high school graduate to a young woman, from a midwestern girl to a well-traveled ingenue, exposed to richness, culture and sophistication. Is that what her mother meant? Marcy squeezed her eyes shut in a fast prayer. Please, let that be what her mother meant. Of course, that must be it.

She breathed more easily, calmer. Her mother had probably detected changes resulting from socio-economic and cultural exposures.

She read on. "*Your daddy and I want you to have these experiences, but don't forget they won't last forever. You will come back to our life, or one like ours.*"

Not if I can help it, Marcy thought defiantly. Not if Daniel will have me.

111

*"Don't forget that you will return to Kurt. You left him as an innocent girl. You must return that way. Or let him think so."*

Marcy's heart lurched to a stop. Her mother had guessed. Everything she'd said had been leading up to this. It was just one small paragraph, but she knew her mother had somehow detected the change. She wiped her suddenly wet palms on her skirt.

*"Do not do anything you can't explain,"* the letter ended.

Of course, she had signed her name. But that was all.

Marcy's trembling hand dropped the paper to the floor. Could Kurt tell also? She knew she could trust her mother to say nothing to him, to keep her secret, but had she, somehow, unwittingly, let out the secret of the men in her life?

Marcy shut her eyes in recollection. God, Kurt would die if he knew how impure she'd been. And yet, it felt so right for her to be doing those things.

She leaned against the wall as she thought of Daniel's lips caressing her shoulders, lapping at her breasts, her belly and thighs. She thought of bending over Yves to taste his passion. And Mrs. Van Couvering's tiny, doll-like body arching rhythmically against her own.

But her mother had warned her: don't do these things if you don't want to get caught.

"But do I care?" Marcy wondered aloud. "I have Daniel, and these things are all right with him." She swallowed nervously, remembering the phrase her mother always used, something about not burning bridges.

She was roused by the maid announcing Yves' arrival as well as a message from Mr. Van Couvering. The driver would call for her at 5:00 to bring her to his office where Daniel would join them and Mrs. Van Couvering for dinner at Lucas-Carton, a fashionable, four-star restaurant.

Shaking her head to push away the unwelcome thoughts, Marcy raced down the stairs to greet Yves.

They roamed the Boulevard de la Madeleine toward the Opera. She tucked her arm in his, feeling sisterly toward him, glad to while away the time. Together, they stopped in the Trois Quartiers where she purchased a much-needed scarf which she immediately wrapped around her neck on the surprisingly cold day. At the Place de l'Opera, they paused in front of the leather, gift and jewelery stores before lunching at the Cafe de la Paix for a *baguette* and a soda.

Despite the brisk day, they chose not to tour the Opera House where they could be warm, but to continue walking toward the Place Vendome. Awed, Marcy stood before the 17th century buildings, enraptured. There, she saw the house where Chopin died and the home of Dr. Mesmer, who discovered mesmerism.

Marcy and Yves lingered in front of Van Cleef & Arpels jewelers, Boucheron and Chaument, her mouth watering at the sight of the luxuries. It was a far cry from High Flats.

"I think we need to go back, Yves. It's almost 4:00, and I will be called for soon," Marcy eventually said, as if she were sad. Actually, her heart hammered at the prospect. For soon she would see Daniel.

"Ah, I wanted to show you more," he said regretfully. *"Eh bien,* another day."

Marcy nodded, but she knew the days were numbered.

Yves hailed a taxi that sped them back to the Van Couverings' home. It was past 4:30 when she reached her room. Speedily, she unpeeled her clothes and dashed into the shower. While she didn't feel particularly gritty, she did want to be her very best for Daniel. Tonight would be their first night in Paris together. Hastily she changed into the other silk blouse and slipped into the skirt.

As she shut the door to her room, she noticed her mother's letter carefully placed in the corner of the desk. The maid must have picked it up and put it there when she tidied the room. Marcy winced in remembrance. Maybe that was one letter she ought not save in her packet. Too revealing.

"Ah, Daniel," she breathed as he showed her his large office overlooking most of Paris. The last sunshine of day had long faded, and now Marcy looked into the distance at a city set off by lights.

"Do you see the Madeleine? And the Eiffel Tower? Look to your left." Daniel placed his hands on either side of her face, directing her toward the building. "There, to your right, is the Louvre. Les Invalides, Napoleon's tomb."

Even as he touched her, a splash of heat surged through her. She didn't want to study geography. She'd rather use it as a backdrop for studying him. Would he take her back to his apartment after dinner? Some discreet hotel? Would he ask to return to the Van Couverings?

"It's beautiful," she said, still staring out, as she thought she was expected to do. How long would they be here?

Daniel closed the door behind him. "M. Van Couvering is in a conference now. He will be free in about an hour. Mme. Van Couvering will be here about 6:00." He spread his hands. "I apologize. I am a poor substitute for my employer."

Marcy's heart beat faster as she turned to look at the walls of glass around her. She swallowed, breathing deeply, trying to quell her trembling. "Oh, not at all."

"Do you like our offices? We have the 28th and 29th floors in this building." Daniel walked over to his large, teak wood desk and began to straighten a pile of papers in front of his chair. "Can I get you something? Some Perrier?"

Unbidden, he walked toward a corner bar, hidden behind two doors that looked like cabinets. He poured a glass of the sparkling water.

115

As he walked toward her, holding it out with one hand, his other reached for her elbow, gently propelling her closer. Marcy gasped sharply, a sudden wetness between her thighs.

Daniel kissed her mouth lightly. "It's always good to see you and have a little time to ourselves, don't you think?"

"Yes, it is," Marcy murmured into his lips. She waited, hoping for more. For as much as she longed to feel his hard body against hers, she was hypnotized by his presence. She could do nothing but wait.

She didn't wait for long. With sudden, quick force, his mouth met hers and slid her waiting lips apart, thrusting his tongue deeply between into her mouth. He pressed his body into hers until she felt his manhood rise against her. Marcy gasped in a hot flush, wondering what next, where could they possibly go from here.

Daniel leaned to the left slightly and placed her Perrier glass on the desk. He edged her back against the double-plated glass window. Urgently, he placed a hand on her breast, squeezing it until her nipples were hard with craving. He kissed her deeply again, as she opened her mouth to receive him.

Marcy ran her fingers over his head and neck, softly fiddling with the skin at the nape. Then, slowly, almost carelessly, she dropped her hand to his groin and rubbed the bulging member. Swiftly, unthinkingly, knowing only that she had to possess it, she unbuttoned his pants and withdrew it. In turn, he lifted her skirt, pulled down her silk panties and hastily inserted himself between her ready and willing loins.

Over and over, they jammed against each other, as he fingered her breasts with one hand and kneaded her anus with the other. Marcy gripped his shoulders, hurling herself against him harder than she thought possible.

The sudden explosion came, shooting through her limbs with greater force than she'd known. She stood panting, propped against the window in exhilaration.

"A 'quickie', as they say in America," Daniel laughed softly. "Well worth it."

"I think all of Paris could see us," Marcy replied, as she ran her fingers across his chest.

"Ah, no, all of Paris was making love also, at the very same time."

Marcy giggled and fondly watched him replace his member in his pants. Teasingly, she bent down and gave its tip a farewell kiss. What fun they would have as the years went by.

"Ah, then, for me too," Daniel responded, bending over. He pulled Marcy's panties down to her knees again and kissed the mound before him. Gently, he inserted his tongue, as his fingers once more kneaded the flesh around her anus.

Again, Marcy felt herself moist with desire. She rolled her pelvis in rhythm to his playful tongue and pressed her outstretched palms on his shoulders. His tongue darted in and out, toying with her sensitive knob. Her gut tightened, and she groaned in delight as the fire cascaded through her.

"Oh, please, please," she wailed softly as she writhed against him, and dug her palms into his shoulders for support until the passion subsided.

Marcy sank to the floor, satisfied and surprised by the depth of her desire. Now she saw his crotch bursting forth as it had earlier. She freed his member, then bent down, and fondling his shaft with her lips, cradled his scrotum with her cupped hand until the hot moisture flooded her mouth.

They lay tangled in each other's bodies and clothes by the giant windows. Only the buzzing intercom roused them from their languor.

"Ah," Daniel scrambled to stand. "Ah, *oui*," he said calmly into the intercom, as if he ordinarily engaged in these kinds of pursuits during business hours. *"Un moment."* He nodded toward Marcy, who struggled to twist her skirt into the proper position and tuck in her shirt again.

Then they joined the Van Couverings for cocktails and dinner. The four spoke in soft, dignified tones. As Mr. Van Couvering addressed Daniel, she wondered if either of them knew of her involvement with the other. Did either care? They treated her so courteously, so solicitously that she suspected that she was a valued friend to them both.

But Marcy wanted more than just friendship

118

with Daniel. She finally knew that she felt about him the same way she had felt about Kurt. Now, however, Kurt seemed like puppy love. They had both been so inexperienced when they swore their love for one another. She now knew that true love could only be built around sexual intimacy also. And she had discovered that with the man who sat next to her, occasionally running his hand up her inner thigh.

"Yes, that would be nice," she nodded in agreement as Daniel offered to escort her to the Lido, the showgirl extravaganza.

"We're going to have a hard time returning you to Delaware," Mr. Van Couvering smiled.

"I don't think Delaware's the problem," countered Marcy. "The midwest might be a little harder." Her small house, just out of town, flashed through her mind. She saw the two backyard horses, the brush-hogged fields, the empty corn crib where they slept on hot summer nights.

"How can a country house replace the streets of romance and bright lights?" quizzed Mr. Van Couvering.

"Your home is so beautiful and peaceful it could replace anything." Except Daniel. Of course, she'd finish her year with the Van Couverings. But then she would return to him, to Paris.

Mr. and Mrs. Van Couvering each kissed the sides of her cheeks goodnight before they headed to their waiting car, and Marcy and Daniel strolled to the Lido.

Daniel slipped the usher a folded note, and Marcy found herself among the very front tables on the dance floor to watch the late night glitz. Daniel ordered a bottle of champagne.

"To the future," Daniel said, clinking his glass against Marcy's.

"To our future," Marcy corrected. She took a small, tentative sip before replacing her glass.

After the show, Daniel escorted Marcy back to his apartment for a night of unending intimacy on the plush rugs before his living room fireplace. He drank champagne, she Perrier, and then they rolled upon each other. He groaned, savoring the soft feel and gentle smell of her flesh until the first glimmerings of day.

Only the distant ringing of the telephone, which he didn't answer, marred the evening.

Marcy spent the next couple of afternoons touring the city with Yves, and the nights with Daniel. In the mornings, when he would drop her off at the mansion before he went to work, she would sleep. When, she wondered, did he?

She'd never been happier. Her letters home read like Michelin guidebooks, enumerating sights, restaurants, exhibits, the weather, the shops. Nothing, though, about her escorts, nothing about her dizzy joy or radiant lust.

"And will you join us for New Year's Eve? We would like that." Mrs. Van Couvering stood next to Marcy in the gray and black kitchen as they sipped Perrier in the early afternoon.

"But I know nothing about this," said Marcy plaintively, for Daniel had not spoken about this. "What is it? What do I wear? Will everyone have dates?" Marcy heard the two refrigerators begin to hum.

"You can wear the crepe dress from the Bergerac evening, an excellent choice. And, of course, not everyone will have a date. This is just a large, festive celebration for close friends of our host and hostess. You will feel comfortable there, and are welcome to spend the entire time with us." Mrs. Van Couvering spoke confidently.

She hesitated. Something nagged her. Why hadn't Daniel said something about this? Maybe he wasn't invited, although it was quite clear that he and the Van Couverings traveled in the same social circle. Perhaps he would be out of town, visiting his parents for the holidays. But, given the amount of time they were together, shouldn't he have mentioned his absence? She placed her empty glass on the granite counter top.

Mrs. Van Couvering noticed Marcy's reflections. "Remember, Marcy, the point of your year here is to acquire experience, see and do as much as you possibly can. Just the existence alone of such an event ought to justify your coming."

Marcy nodded. "You're right. I'm sorry. I just felt sort of lost for a second." She didn't mention her concerns about Daniel.

Mrs. Van Couvering reached out and took

Marcy's hand. "I miss you, Marcy. We miss not seeing you, but understand that you cannot possibly fit everything in right now," she said discreetly. She placed her glass on the counter also and looked up directly at the younger woman before nodding and leaving the kitchen, her heels clicking against the stone floors.

Now Marcy stood in front of her floor length mirror, contemplating the dress that captured the sumptuous breasts and slim waist. Mrs. Van Couvering could not have done better in buying this, Marcy mused, setting the clasp in her blonde mane. After hours of practice, she'd mastered the art of putting up her tresses.

Tonight would be the first night in several that she'd not been with Daniel, not felt his strong hold on her limbs, his engorged sex between her legs. She bit her lip to erase the memory and headed down the hall to the staircase.

Mr. Van Couvering bowed slightly from the bottom as she edged down the steps, daintily placing her feet, clad in her black pumps, on the treads.

"Lovely, Marcy, a true vision," he commented.

"Thank you." She stood beside him, about to ask him who the hosts were, when she stopped in awe. For Mrs. Van Couvering had just begun her descent in a vibrant, one-shouldered red dress that swathed her body in luxurious folds of fabric.

"And, you, my darling, are ravishing." Mr. Van Couvering stepped forward and kissed his wife's cheek in admiration.

Then they headed for the car.

The New Year's Eve party, given by the Heil-bruns, spanned two floors of their Parisian town-house: the ballroom and the indoor swimming pool. Bright strings of colored lights hung like gar-lands above the waters, reflecting the shimmering dresses of the women and the handsome square jaws of the men.

Marcy smiled fondly as she remembered telling Mrs. Van Couvering and Daniel how she liked anything in water. But, tonight, she felt suddenly vulnerable. She stood close by her employers, eye-ing the crowd, trying to distinguish Daniel among the tuxedoed men. But there was no sign of him. How had he disappeared so mysteriously? She dared not ask Mr. Van Couvering, for fear he would think her too cloying or, worse, too aggres-sive.

After some minutes, she was emboldened. She headed for a table of hors d'oeuvres. Black caviar, tiny shrimp, smoked salmon and oysters gleamed from their ice-studded platters.

"Oh, *excusez-moi,*" Marcy mumbled as she stepped on a pointed black shoe.

"Ah, all right, it's all right," a lush, deep, heavily accented French voice replied, clearly aware that an American had just apologized to her.

Marcy turned to regard its owner, a black-haired woman, slightly older than she was, with long hair, past her shoulders. She was dressed in a low-cut black dress with no jewels save a glimmering diamond on her left ring finger. The woman smiled, but then quickly turned as a friend hugged her and lifted the scarlet-tipped hand with the diamond.

"Ooo-la-la," the admirer squealed, twisting the wrist to better examine the ring.

It must be new, mused Marcy wistfully as she directed her attention toward the smoked salmon. A waited lifted some to her plate.

"Ooo," a gray-haired woman cooed, also lifting the hand to examine the ring. Obviously, she got the ring today or people wouldn't be jumping all over her to see it. Marcy touched her thumb to her left ring finger. Empty. Of course, what could she expect so soon?

Marcy turned to regard the black-haired woman further. Her makeup was flawless, her features finely chiseled, clearly the product of years of culture, sophistication and good luck.

Her little plate filled by a waiter, Marcy wandered back to the Van Couverings, but they had sauntered off somewhere. Marcy shrugged, only vaguely uncomfortable. At least no one was paying attention to her. She didn't feel like a wallflower as much as an unnoticed fly on the wall. She picked up her wine glass filled with Perrier and headed out of the poolroom to inspect the ballroom, dressed for dancing.

Suddenly, her heart thumped with joy. For there, not five feet before her was Daniel. She'd recognize the powerful back anywhere. Daniel. She opened her mouth to call out to him.

And then she stopped, her lips apart, her hand poised midair in greeting. She didn't move. Yes, there was Daniel all right, in the far corner, by a small winding iron staircase. And, there, also, was the black-haired girl with the ring. His arm encircled her waist.

He leaned over and kissed her cheek, then ran his fingers up her bare back to her neck, which he gracefully cupped in his hand.

Marcy stumbled against the wall, gasping. The girl raised her elegant finger tips to his lips and he kissed them also. As he had often kissed hers. He slipped his arm down, resting his hand comfortably on her shapely buttocks.

Then, as Marcy looked at him, he bent forward and kissed the girl deeply on the lips. Her fingers entwined themselves in his hair as she pulled his head closer toward her. His hand rose to her head again and gently pulled her hair, throwing her head back as he gazed at her. He murmured something, then bent forward again for another deeply probing kiss.

No one could see them, except Marcy. She could not remove her eyes. Daniel ran his hands over her back and around her small buttocks, scooping them upward. His other hand now rested lightly on the swelling over her low-cut bodice. They pressed against one another, their pelvis rotating in unison. It was clear to Marcy that this was familiar territory. Very, very familiar.

The ring glittered in the lamplight.

Mouth agape, Marcy could only stare, too
horrified to move.

# CHAPTER 9

Marcy's heart lurched into her throat, a steel knife sliced into the core of her stomach. She shook her head in abject disbelief and agony at the sight before her.

She clutched her throat with her hand. What should I do, she panicked. Ask him? See if this was a mistake? An old girlfriend, a cousin, a friend, perhaps? But she knew, knew as certainly as if a banner had been strung overhead. She gasped for breath, her hand grasping her neck. She pressed back against the wall to keep from reeling over.

Faint, she haltingly walked to a bathroom and swooned against the sill.

Tears blurred her eyes, her breath came in short heaves as she put her hand to her heart trying to still it.

"What should I do?" she whispered as tears gathered in her eyes. "How can I bear it?"

All those dreams crashed around her. How could he do this to me? How could he love someone else? How could he not tell me that there was someone? How could he love someone when it was clear that I loved him? Marcy hung her head, watching tears fall to her lap. Sobbing, she sank to a silk-covered arm chair, her head in her hands.

She swayed back and forth forlornly looking for comfort from somewhere. But there was none.

She didn't know how many minutes had passed, but she knew she had to return to the dance. How long had she hidden here? Someone would want to use this room soon. Mr. Van Couvering might start to ask for her.

Trembling, Marcy stood. Maybe I'm wrong, she gulped, as she dabbed her swollen eyes with a wet towel. No one could be as cruel as he was to me. It must be a mistake. Cheered by that thought, she straightened her dress and left the bathroom.

Marcy pasted a smile on her face as she joined the Van Couverings at their table.

"Oh, we missed you," Mr. Van Couvering said joyously, rising as she sat with them and a few other couples. "Having fun?"

"Yes, very much, sir," Marcy replied, smiling gamely. Did Mr. Van Couvering ask her that to prod her for information? Did he want to know whether she'd seen Daniel yet? Did he know that Daniel had another woman? In vain, her eyes searched the room for Daniel.

"Care to dance?" Mr. Van Couvering inclined his head toward her.

Marcy nodded her assent as Mrs. Van Couvering turned to the man next to her.

Adroitly, holding her lightly yet as firmly as when he intimately fondled her, Mr. Van Couvering danced around the sparkling dance floor, built by the pool's edge. Their reflections shimmered in the water.

Ah, she thought mournfully, it should be so beautiful tonight. Why couldn't this be Daniel? But there was no Daniel, never again. An overwhelming heaviness stole across her, even as she moved in a sprightly step in her employer's arms. Would this evening ever be over? Could she hold back the tears that threatened to engulf her?

"Uh," Marcy drew her breath in sharply.

"Yes?"

"Oh, nothing. It's all—all so beautiful," she managed. She didn't want to tell Mr. Van Couvering her troubles. She didn't really want to know on whose side he would stand. So she said nothing.

As they returned to the table, Marcy excused herself for the bathroom again. She headed down the wide hallway, filled with chatter and laughter of boisterous friends.

"Ah, Marcy."

She stopped, rigid.

"Ah, Marcy." It was Daniel. He came up to her and kissed her cheeks in greeting.

She flushed with relief. Maybe, after all, it was all OK. "I didn't know you were here," she said, tears of happiness flooding her eyes.

"Oh, no?" was all he asked. He turned his head, as if looking for someone. "I wanted to wish you well in the New Year. You will return to the United States in two days, and I may not see you for awhile."

Marcy's mouth dropped open. That was it?

That was what he wanted to say after all their days and nights together? A casual farewell, as if to a co-worker. She stared at him, unable to fathom his rebuff. Daniel leaned over and pecked each cheek.

Marcy clutched at her stomach, as if to grab the lump that suddenly filled it.

"Who was that girl?" she blurted. She had to know.

"Which?" He raised his brows quizzically, and again looked about him.

Marcy swallowed. "Tell me," she whispered frantically. "The one with the diamond ring, the black hair. Who?"

"Simone de Seville."

"Yes?"

"My fiancée."

"Your what?" She stared at him in horror. It was one thing to imagine, but quite another to hear it, to find out that it was really so.

"Ah, yes, didn't I tell you?"

"Why *would* you tell me?" she asked bitterly. "How could it help you if you told me you had a fiancée?"

"Ah, I see."

"Since when? All the time you were making love to me you—you had a fiancée?" She trembled with unexpected indignation.

"No, not at all. Please, understand."

She shook off the hand he placed on her bare arm.

"I have had a fiancée only since noon."

"And last night, when you—you made love to me, you were about to have a fiancée today?" she spat out. "I call that a very fine line. Did you buy the ring this morning? Last night you were a free man, with the scruples of a free man. But now, you're a devoted fiancé?" Marcy's eyes blazed.

"But—"

"Did you make love to me with her approval? Or in secret? Did you alternate? First me, then her? First her, then me? Which?" She grabbed his tuxedoed-covered forearms and dug her strong fingers into them.

"Ah, no, you do not understand." He spoke soothingly.

"Explain it." Marcy's voice hardened. Inside, she longed to have a coherent explanation, one that she could believe, one that would let her take him into her arms and feel his caresses over her body. One that would let her forgive him, when he told her it was all a mistake.

But that would not be.

"She was away. In Monte Carlo."

"You—you—" Marcy searched for the worst word she could think of. "Creep. A cad, a creep and a two-timer." She gritted her teeth and dug her fingers still further into his arms, hoping to give him the pain that had wrapped itself around her like a tight shroud.

"I do not do things like this ordinarily." Daniel slowly removed his arms from Marcy's grasp. "But

131

you seemed to need a friend. You seemed to need a man, a safe man, a man who would not hurt you."

Marcy's chest heaved. "And what do you think you just did? Maybe you didn't hurt me physically, but what about my feelings?"

Her lips trembled with the exertion of restraining her tears. She put her hand on her breast.

"I think you're scum," she seethed. "You led me on so you could get laid!" Marcy reached out and slapped his face. Then she wheeled around and returned to the festivities. It was over. If he had purposefully set out to burn her in a hot flame, he could not have done worse.

Smiling crazily, because she knew that just one chink in her armor would cause her to give way, she danced and chattered the rest of the night, willing her body to fight or until she could return to the sanctity of her room. She smiled engagingly at her dinner partners who then asked her to dance and led her firmly to the dance floor. She pressed her breasts a little too closely during the slower dances, rotated her pelvis a bit too forthrightly during the fast dances. Anything, do anything, just do get through his night.

# Part II

## CHAPTER 10

*"Dear Kurt,"* she wrote, propped against her massive pillows. *"Mrs. Van Couvering, her friend, Alexandra and I returned to Delaware yesterday. Mr. Van Couvering went to London. It is a relief to be back, to see familiar, comfortable surroundings. I didn't know that I missed my steady routine as much as I obviously did. I may not be the world traveler I thought I was."*

Marcy tried to make the letter lighthearted, but she stumbled over each word. Always, weighing heavily upon her, was the abandonment. Even now, when she thought of the rough ending to that night, she shuddered, sobs threatening to wrack her yet again. She bit her lip hard, hoping to dull the pain that gnawed at her every waking minute. Maybe she should have let the incident with Simone pass, as if unnoticed, in the hope that she could have squeezed a final night of love-making. As much as she missed him, she knew she also missed his hands upon her body.

*"I'm not sure what our plans are, but I am crossing out the days til I come home. Six months!"* She placed an exclamation mark, but didn't really feel it. In fact, she didn't really feel much of anything. Then she signed her name, sealed the letter in the waiting envelope, and dropped off to sleep in exhaustion.

*"I'm thinking of flying east in June to pick you up, see where you've been during the year,"* wrote Kurt in his next letter. *"I think this year will have been so important to you that I should have some idea of how you've lived. What do you think? Is there a room in the Van Couverings' house for me to stay? Let me know so I can make reservations now. I can get a cheap flight. Then we can fly home together."*

Marcy's jaw dropped. It had never dawned on her that Kurt might want to see this world. She'd thought this was hers entirely, a secret that she'd be able to keep. If he came out here, then he'd discover everything. How could she hide her relationship with the Van Couverings? Wouldn't he notice her conspiratorial looks with Giselle? Marcy gulped. But if she told him not to come, wouldn't he notice even more?

"What do you think?" She held the letter out to Giselle and Sigrid.

"How fun. You could sneak down the hall at night and slip into his bed," Giselle winked.

"Giselle!" Marcy's eyes widened. "I never even did it with him once!"

"Then you would have a great time. You won't find it as convenient in High Flats when you have to sneak in the back of parked cars and movie theaters."

"I don't think it's as simple as all that," Marcy muttered, looking down. Yes, of course, they were right, he should come. She'd write him tonight to come in June, but it wouldn't be so simple as just conveniently jumping into bed with him now that he was here. For he mustn't find out. Somehow, now that Daniel had wounded her, Kurt seemed especially dear.

Still how could she go from the girl who would hardly let her breasts be touched to the woman who yearned for that touch? At least his arrival was still six months away.

"Anyway," said Sigrid, handing the letter back, "I think you need some body contact now. Wipe out the memories of that awful Daniel."

Marcy nodded. "I know, but I can't. He was wonderful. I loved him," she continued dully. "He was everything."

"Everything rotten," stormed Sigrid. "Imagine how cruel he will be to his wife, how cruel he was to that woman before he became engaged to her."

Marcy stared in sudden recognition. "You're— you're right," she stammered. "I absolutely never thought of that. I thought of how mean he was to me, as a girlfriend. I never considered how mean he would be to me as a wife."

As if hit by a shaft of lightning, the leaden cloud that had weighed her down for weeks immediately lifted. Impulsively, she leaned forward and kissed Sigrid's cheek. "Thank you, thank you so much!"

"Ready to go?" Giselle giggled.

Marcy nodded, suddenly itching to be out and about. "I think I'm a new woman. I can hardly believe that just one sentence has turned my life upside down."

The torment had been so severe that it hardly seemed possible that one phrase had altered her world. Unless, of course, she mused, enough time and distance had occurred so that it was just the right moment to be healed, and it might have happened anyway.

Still, she felt better. At last.

Now, she dressed with care. For when Giselle had asked if she were ready, she meant it. Her friends had marked out a new path for her. Marcy thought it gleamed like the yellow brick road.

She tiptoed around her room, putting on her clothes. Alexandra had chosen to fall asleep in her bed til she returned that night, so she needed to dress cautiously. She scouted about for the Cabochard Mrs. Van Couvering had given her in Paris. Ah, here, under the pile of underwear on her dresser. She dabbed the fragrance on her throat and wrists, turned down the lights and ran downstairs to wait for Sigrid to drive her to Giselle's.

She giggled with expectation. She hadn't felt so good in weeks, suddenly free of all the unhappiness that had dogged her. Giselle's boyfriend would bring a friend from the university whom he assured Marcy she would like. She hoped so, she surely needed to like someone special. For, now suddenly lighthearted again, she missed the attentions of Mr. Van Couvering, who was still away, and Mrs. Van Couvering, who was out nightly with her guest.

Marcy smiled, genuinely pleased to meet the tall, husky, brown-haired Mike standing before her. He had the powerful shoulders of a football player and the big, sappy grin of a nice guy.

The six sat around Giselle's rooms in a carriage house, separate from the main house, where she was free to entertain. While Marcy wasn't sure she'd like to live in the three bedroom cottage apart from the rest of the family, she now recognized its advantages as they played Pictionary and listened to music.

There was a lull in the conversation. Giselle's angular boyfriend, Whit, stood and pulled her to her feet. "Will you excuse us," he grinned, leading her away.

Then Sigrid stumbled to her feet. "If you don't mind?" She and her friend, Larry, also left the room.

Now Marcy and Mike sat, side by side, facing the still open game of Pictionary and the Pepsi bottle and empty glasses on the wood table in front of them. Marcy looked down in embarrassment. It was clear what the others were going to do. What about her and Mike? She looked at the muscular thighs propped up next to hers. She eyed the powerful arms covered with black hair resting on his knees.

Instantly, she knew what she wanted to do. But would he ask her? Would he know about the third bedroom upstairs, the one with the bed in the alcove and the yellow painted walls?

Her heart pumping, she waited anxiously, feeling her breath becoming more labored.

"Marcy?" his softly Southern voice asked.

She looked up, and felt his gentle arms around her, pulling her lips to his. He kissed her softly and ran his hands over her back and shoulders, carefully avoiding her breasts. He's probably as nervous as I am, she said to herself.

Marcy buried her face in his neck, then turned to meet his lips with her own. His tongue toyed with the edges of her mouth, prancing in and out. His hands rested on her shoulders, as if content to remain there all night.

But Marcy knew she wanted more. And though she waited patiently for his hands to roam and his kisses to meander, at last she had to take matters into her own hands. She took one of his hands and placed it on her firm breast. Mike responded by massaging it gently. Eagerly, Marcy pulled his T-shirt out of his jeans and ran her fingers lightly over his hairy chest.

With sudden urgency, he pulled her cotton shirt out of her skirt and reached upward to cup both her breasts in his hands. He moaned. Marcy looked down kindly, brushing her face against his thick hair. He pulled her shirt higher as he tried to unclasp her dainty bra.

"Not here," she murmured, standing. "Upstairs." She stood, he stood, and she eyed his swollen member arching against his faded jeans. Unable to restrain herself, she placed her hand on it, rubbing it gently. He moaned again, as she rubbing him over and over. He tried to pull her toward him, but she stayed far enough away that he could only fondle her breasts.

Then, Marcy, taking his hand, led him upstairs. At the top of the landing, she stopped and turned toward him teasingly. Carefully, she ran her forefinger down his fly, feeling his turgid member within. She rolled her hand over the jeans and then swiftly unbuckled his belt. Without moving, she placed her hand on his navel, rubbing it til he rolled his eyes and again groaned.

He reached for her, drawing her closer to him. Swiftly, he ran his hand up her inner thigh, stopping at the soft, fleshy part near her mound. Gently, he massaged it, as she swiveled her hips toward him. Tenderly, he touched her vulva til Marcy squirmed with delight, even as she lightly ran her fingers over his stomach and ribs.

Then, alluringly, she turned and headed down

the small hallway toward the room. She grinned as she heard Giselle's bed squeaking on its old springs. That bed was probably never intended for her exploits, she thought. And the one I use will probably fall on top of us. She closed the door to the yellow room and turned to face him.

Unable to wait, Mike unbuttoned her blouse quickly and grasped Marcy's breasts in his hands. "Great," he murmured, dipping his fingers inside the cups and lifting out the entire breasts so that they hung before him like oranges. Swiftly, Marcy unzipped his pants, and lifted his swollen member out of his underwear. She stared in delight at its spectacular size.

Hastily, they undressed each other, then stood, separate, admiring the other's body. He brushed his fingers against her silken skin til she quivered with lust. Then, unexpectedly, Mike wrapped his arms around Marcy's waist and lifted her up. She wrapped her legs around his hips and pressed against him, listening to him grunt, feeling the heat mount within herself, until he inserted his member. They heaved against each other, her legs clamped tightly around him until they came in unison.

"Great, you're great." Mike said, gently sliding Marcy to the floor.

"You too. That was fun." Wide-eyed, Marcy glanced at his member, still engorged. "Looks like you could do it again." Her eyes twinkled.

"Try me." Mike sat on the edge of the bed, his

140

manhood thrusting upward. "Sit here," he pointed.

"Really?" Marcy wriggled on top of him, fully inserting the hilt. "Oh, great," she shivered, as a wave of heat swelled over her.

She'd never done it again so quickly. Usually there was a wait of some time. Resting on his large weapon, she gradually began to rotate her pelvis, til she felt him swelling inside her even further. He buried his face between her breasts and pinched her nipples. Marcy gripped his back and moved faster and faster, until the explosion rocked them both.

Panting, she fell against him as he fell backward onto the bed.

"Again?" she giggled, pulling away.

For an answer, he kissed her hard, so her teeth dug into her lips. He reached a hand up and toyed with her nipples til they grew taut. He inserted his finger into her vulva and moved it til Marcy squealed for more. Delighted, she saw his already tumid manhood, propped up like a giant nail. She shivered with expectation as she again felt the moisture between her legs.

Marcy bent over, her lips poised on the end of the shaft. Mike placed his hands on her hips, guiding her on top of him again. She slid on top of his shaft and rotated her hips til they were thoroughly spent. Finally, she rolled over onto the bed. "I feel as if I just splurged on a banana split," she giggled. "I never had so much at once."

When the six met downstairs again, they were each flushed and giggly.

"How about Thursday?" Giselle offered. "Maybe a little Nintendo?"

But Marcy turned out to be busy.

Mr. Van Couvering arrived home that afternoon with Lord Worthington, a tall, graying aristocratic gentleman, a member of the House of Lords, as his father had been. He and Mr. Van Couvering had done business for years, as their fathers had done before them.

Marcy was invited to join them for dinner. Hastily, she put Alexandra to bed, reading her about Paddington the Bear, and lightly kissing her cheek. Alexandra snuggled into her sheets and covers and immediately fell asleep.

Relieved that she wouldn't have to sit with her, Marcy raced off to her room to slip on her black skirt and white silk blouse. She put her hair up with the clasp Mrs. Van Couvering had given her, then twirled in the mirror admiring the effect: glamorous and somewhat sophisticated. That was precisely what she hoped would happen.

From under her long lashes, Marcy sneaked glances at Mr. Van Couvering at the dinner table. She had missed him, missed that sinewy, lanky body and the long, expert fingers. When would he knock for her again? She pressed her thighs together as she felt that familiar tingling begin at the thought of him on top of her.

Swiftly, she turned toward Lord Worthington opposite her seat, and found him looking frankly at her. She smiled back, admiring the craggy face and square jaw, below a full head of graying hair. She felt her nipples harden as she pressed her thighs together still tighter. This was absurd. He was older than her boss and a Lord, to boot, she admonished herself. No point getting hot over him. She wiggled against the burgundy seat covers. Perhaps she would be free after dinner and could call Mike to her service.

But there was no need to.

Shortly after Mrs. Van Couvering and her guest left for a concert in Philadelphia, Marcy heard the familiar tap on her door. She puzzled, wondering if Lord Worthington had retired for the evening. She put down her mystery and stood, straightening her skirt as Mr. Van Couvering entered the room.

"It's so good to see you, Marcy." He stretched out a hand. "Have you resolved your difficulties?"

She nodded, knowing that he alluded to Daniel. And then, she nodded emphatically again, for at the sight of Mr. Van Couvering, she knew she finally had. She came to him, and without waiting, planted her lips on his, and pushed her tongue against him until he opened his mouth for her. She pressed against him.

"Marcy," he murmured into her ear.

She nodded, her breath beginning to come quickly.

"Lord Worthington." He needn't have said

anything more, for she knew instantly. He wanted her to go to him. She'd never had a man that age before. And after someone like Mike, she wondered if Lord Worthington would be any match. "Come, then."

Mr. Van Couvering walked down the hall to the guest wing. Marcy followed him into Lord Worthington's quarters. Surprised, she watched as Mr. Van Couvering shut the door to the room. Would he just stay for the introductions? Or would he watch? She stood facing Lord Worthington who was dressed in a navy satin smoking jacket, reading in the wing chair by the window. He stood in greeting.

"Marcy," he spoke in the clipped accent she had admired at dinner. He stepped forward. "I am delighted you are here."

"Thank you, sir," she replied. And she was. She wondered why Mr. Van Couvering remained. But as she heard him slip out of his jacket, she knew. Then she heard him pull his tie out of the collar. She stood, wondering what to do next.

But Mr. Van Couvering knew what to do. He came up from behind and placed his hands on her breasts. She drew her breath in quickly, for his touch was so deft that it pricked at the flesh beneath her silk blouse and lace bra. Through the fabrics, he began to toy with her nipples, running his fingers round and round. She opened her thighs slightly, feeling the moisture between her legs begin to spread. Still standing motionless, she

144

watched Lord Worthington take off his smoking jacket and his pants.

"Oh, I say," he muttered, bending over to take off his shoes. He unfastened the garters that held his socks to his calf. She saw his buttocks tighten as he bent. She reached behind her and placed her hand on Mr. Van Couvering's hardening member. As she caressed it, she felt Lord Worthington place a hand between her thighs and run it up to her genitalia.

Marcy writhed with pleasure, pushing against the fingers that gently probbed her. Swiftly, she slipped out of her skirt and underclothes. But she let Mr. Van Couvering continue to toy with her breasts through her blouse. Lord Worthington dropped to his knees and began to kiss her mons til Marcy gasped. With one hand she rubbed Mr. Van Couvering's hard member, the other she ran through Lord Worthington's hair as she groaned with delight.

Lord Worthington stood and unbuttoned her blouse, then her bra. Mr. Van Couvering dropped his fingers to her buttocks, kneading them and her genitals. Lord Worthington's tongue fiddled with her nipples. She reached down and grasped his hard member, delicately touching it. His tongue worked more furiously on her breasts as she skimmed her fingers along his shaft.

Soon Lord Worthington led her to the queen-sized bed and placed her down. She lay, wriggling and breathing heavily as the men pawed at her, fondling every inch of her voluptuous body. Her hair fell from the clasp and lay about her in thick stands as the two men licked and kissed her thoroughly.

Finally, when she thought she could stand the suspense no longer, Mr. Van Couvering lay on his back, and guided her to her knees so that she straddled him, her mouth directly over his pulsating manhood. She took it deeply between her lips. Lord Worthington mounted her from behind. He ran his hands over her body, and placed his hardness between her legs and anus, til it found its rightful place. He pushed against her. Marcy groaned with pleasure. It seemed never to have felt so good. All parts of her were satiated, all parts were working. She reached back and fondled the Lord's scrotum til he grunted and pushed harder against her. He ran his hand over her stomach and placed his fingers in her navel til she began to heave backward against him. All the while, she mouthed at Mr. Van Couvering's manhood.

Moving her entire body as she never had, feeling the two opposite pressures, Marcy strained against each man until she felt the three of them explode forcefully. She fell forward onto Mr. Van Couvering, even as Lord Worthington toppled on her. The three lay in a heap, panting silently.

"Is this international business?" Marcy asked gaily.

"The best there is," replied Lord Worthington,

as he stood and stretched upward. He winked at her.

Quickly, she showered and dressed to join the two men. They had opened a bottle of Dom Perignon, but Marcy merely removed a club soda from the small frig in the room. They toasted one another happily.

Lord Worthington stayed the week, and Marcy and Mr. Van Couvering joined him in the evenings in his quarters to replay their first encounter. During the day, she thought of nothing more than Lord Worthington whose dignity and grace charmed her, whose touch ignited her. Vaguely, she wondered what life would be like when he returned to England the following day. Of course, she'd never been alone with him, but she could tell from their varied positions that he would have been a sensuous single mate.

She dropped the mystery she was reading at the tap on her door. She glanced at the clock. Of course, 9:30; this was when Mr. Van Couvering generally came by.

"Hello, Marcy. A difficulty tonight."

"Oh?" she said in consternation. She'd really looked forward to it.

"I've gotten a sudden emergency and need to spend some time on the phone with Japan now. But Lord Worthington would like it if you would join him in any case."

"Oh? Sure." What luck. She closed her door and strode down the halls to his room. His door

147

was open.

"I say, I'm a lucky chap that you'd come see me alone." He smiled, and offered her a glass of club soda in a champagne glass.

Marcy nodded her thanks and eagerly shut the door behind her. She eyed him in his navy smoking jacket and smoke gray pants. What dignity he exuded.

"Rotten about that call to Japan, I'm afraid," Lord Worthington continued.

"We'll miss him, but we'll be OK, don't you think?"

In reply, Lord Worthington winked. He put down his glass, took Marcy's, and swiftly undressed them both. They stood in the middle of the large room, facing the window that overlooked the swimming pool.

"Can't wait til we can swim again," she said, walking to the window. She parted the heavy draperies and peered out at the darkness. She could just make out the black winter cover loaded down with leaves that closed the pool for the winter. It really was barren she thought, that vast black hole out there.

Lord Worthington came up behind her, placing his hands on her hips, his penis resting in the space between her buttocks. She wriggled against it, waiting for it to harden. Still watching the night, she reached behind and placed her hand on his stomach. She heard him quickly draw in his breath. Then she felt the first tinges of the hardness which she awaited. As she pressed against him, feeling him grow between her cheeks, she grew wet with desire. She placed her thumb in his navel, as he did the same to her. He moved it around, and with his other hand, pressed the sides together, forming a sort of vulva. Marcy arched forward and then back.

She turned toward the Lord's smiling face and kissed his lips. With his tongue, he forced open her mouth and kissed her deeply. His member pressed against her stomach, as his fingers kneaded her behind, spreading it wider and wider.

They pressed against each other until he led her to the bed. She quivered with excitement, imagining his hard rod jamming her. She bit her lip trying to calm herself.

He bent her in the familiar position, up on her knees, so that he could enter from behind. In this position, her breasts swung free from her body, and he seemed to relish their size.

Wet, she waited, spreading her legs. Yes, she knew the drill. And she loved it. She knew he'd place one hand on a breast and gently pinch a nipple. With the other he would massage her taut stomach and her genitals til she thought she couldn't bear it. Then, as she writhed with heat, he would plunge his manhood deeper and deeper inside her.

He came behind her, as she knew, but instead of placing his member to her vulva, he brought it to her behind. He pressed against it.

"No, please," Marcy said. That was not for her. She didn't need a moment's thought. She didn't want this. She wouldn't have this.

"It shan't hurt." He tightened his grip around her waist, intending that she not move. He pressed his shaft against her further.

"No, I said, no," she spoke softly but firmly.

"It's quite common, you know," he panted, pushing harder.

Marcy tried to pull away, but he held her tightly. His tip pressed against her cheeks, trying to ply them apart.

"Ah, rot, you're tight," he muttered, not giving up.

"I said, no, absolutely no," Marcy tried to wriggle away, but she couldn't move, caught in his vice-like grip. "Please, oh, please," she begged, trying to break free.

But she couldn't do it. He pushed her head down so that her buttocks were poised upward like the top of a children's slide.

"Oh, please, no," she pleaded. "Not that."

She cried out as he pressed and separated a little bit more.

"Be quiet," he ordered. He tried to widen her, but she clenched her buttocks together. It hurt where he prodded and poked at her.

"Sit still, damn it," he ordered, beginning to insert himself.

Marcy groaned, as the pain began. She moved this way and that, pulling, pushing, trying to break free, as he pressed her opening harder.

Then suddenly, she lifted her strong, farm girl's leg and heaved it backward, planting her foot firmly against his stomach, propelling him off her.

She jumped up, her chest heaving, all desire gone. "No, I said, no, never, absolutely never!" She yelled out, scrambling to her feet to face him.

He reached down, briefly catching her leg. But with one swift movement, she shot up her knee to hit him in the groin. He caught her leg, tripping her. Now he grabbed her arm. With tight fingers, he dragged her toward him. Marcy tried to yank her arm free and sidestep him, but he held her tightly, and he placed her squarely in front of him.

"You bitch," he muttered. "You'll do it my way."

Afraid, Marcy struggled against him, no longer strong enough to fight back. What happened to the aristocratic older man? Now she faced a violent, perverted one. Could Mr. Van Couvering have known? But she didn't have time to think.

He pulled her toward the bed again and forced her on her stomach. He sat on her back and edged down her buttocks, past her thighs onto her legs.

"You'll know what buggery is now, won't you?" he gritted his teeth.

"No, I said, no. And I will not have it," Marcy cried out, her legs flailing. It was no use. He pushed against her as he changed his position.

And, then, suddenly, Marcy knew what to do.

She remembered Giselle once telling. She remembered: she was to lay passively, as if she would cooperate. And then spring.

"OK, I'll do it," she muttered, closing her eyes. She relaxed, stopped fighting. He released her arms. And just as quickly, gathering all the speed and fire she possessed, Marcy turned over frontward, and sharply plucked her fingers into his eyes. He reeled backward. With her two fists together, she pounded him in the groin, til he fell back. She slid her feet out from beneath him, free finally.

Hurriedly, as he lay moaning, clutching his hands to his crotch, she jumped up, grabbed her clothes and ran to her room. She slammed the door, locked and leaned against it, panting with relief and fear. Tears flooded her eyes, her chest heaved.

"What happened?" she asked herself, bewildered. "How did it go from such niceness to such awful ugliness?" She closed her eyes, reliving the night. Was she right? Should she have done what he wanted? Surely Mr. Van Couvering would rebuke her. Should she return, apologetically? But even as she stood, still crying, still panting, she knew she'd been right. She should do what she wanted. Certainly, she was liberal enough in her activities that most people were satisfied. But she would never, never do something so repugnant to her.

Slowly, it dawned on her how successfully she had eluded him. Stupefied, she looked at her strong hands, still holding her clothes, hands that she'd always disliked for their very strength, and realized that they had saved her, realized that she had the ability to save herself.

Grimly, she wondered what she'd say to her mother in tonight's letter.

# CHAPTER 11

It was an aberrant spring day, the beginning of April when the seasons toyed with everyone: two days of warmth and pale green buds, a peeping snowdrop, then ten days of bone-chilling cold.

But not today. Today, Marcy was outside, sitting on the grass just turning green from the hay-color of winter. She slipped off her pumps and rolled her bare toes in the grass. In the far off lawn, near the paths through the woods, Alexandra and her friend Jessica romped, closely tracked by Giselle and Whit.

Marcy smiled at Mike, opposite her, leaning against a tree. They'd seen each other frequently, when he didn't have school and she had no particular plans with Alexandra. Sometimes the three of them would play ball or Chutes & Ladders or watch a video tape. Sometimes he'd just come over to watch Marcy read to the child or bake brownies. Marcy was comfortable with him and now, as she smiled, she thought vaguely about staying on. He had another year of college. She was sure the Van Couverings would let her spend another year with them.

It was hard to remember if Kurt were right for her anymore. He wanted to be a farmer, Mike wanted to be an engineer. Kurt wanted five kids, Mike didn't know. Kurt wanted to stay in the midwest, Mike wanted to stay in the east. Yes, she was happy with both. They were kind, considerate, fun, interesting. Well, she shrugged, she wouldn't worry about it now. It was too lovely a day. But she'd have to think about it soon because Kurt was flying to Philadelphia in a couple months.

Even if nothing panned out with Kurt, it was a relief to have him in her life after that disgusting Lord. At least Mike had normal sexual inclinations, none of that filthy buggery stuff. Marcy wrinkled her nose in disgust at the remembrance of him.

She'd been nervous the day after her experience, making sure that she would not run across him that morning. While she certainly didn't want to see him, she was particularly concerned that he might have said something to Mr. Van Couvering which would make him angry. Or, perhaps worse, that he'd said nothing and Mr. Van Couvering would expect the threesome again. Oh, well, in that case, she'd pretend to be sick after dinner.

But nothing happened. In the late morning, he had left. The butler had brought down his bags, Lawrence had lifted them into the car and they had sped off.

"Isn't he leaving suddenly?" Marcy gulped when she saw Mr. Van Couvering at the front door. She had to know if Lord Worthington had said anything and if Mr. Van Couvering were angry.

"Yes, he said he had urgent business." He eyed Marcy quizzically, pursed his lips, but said nothing.

And Marcy knew that Mr. Van Couvering knew something had happened last night that led to the Lord's abrupt departure, and that he chose not to discuss it. Perhaps these sorts of things had happened before. Perhaps he knew that Marcy had certain standards that could not be upset. She was thankful not to discuss it. She knew she couldn't be calm and matter-of-fact, for the thought of him still repulsed her.

But as long as that night didn't come between her and her employer, then she would be pleased.

And she'd had enough nights afterward to prove that it hadn't.

Now, Marcy glanced at the far lawn and saw the two children and two adults skipping through the grass, all holding hands. Marcy watched Mike leaning against the tree, his eyes closed, knees bent, feeling the day. She stuck her leg out from her billowing blue skirt and touched her toes to the space between his legs. He bolted upright.

"Hey, what are you doing?" he grinned, pulled himself up, and tried to close his legs so she'd remove her foot.

"Nothing, why?" she answered, quite seriously. "Sit back. Come on."

Mike hesitated.

"Oh, come on, no one can see. They're miles

away, and I'm looking at them." Marcy's toes danced on the seam of his faded jeans.

"Hey, when did you get red toe nails?"

"Wednesday. Sigrid painted them. What do you think?"

"Nice." He grabbed her foot, but she wouldn't stop her movements. Languidly, he let his muscular hand rest on her ankle as she massaged his member repeatedly. Fascinated, as always, she watched the bulge begin.

"Ok, you better stop now, Marcy," Mike said hoarsely.

"Nope, don't worry. They're still out there."

"Marce, I can't stand this much longer."

"Then don't. Just go with it." More forcefully, she rubbed her toes against him til she saw him jerk and press back hard against the tree, tightening his hold on her ankle.

She smiled benignly. "Nice?"

"Yeah." He smiled. "What about you?"

"I'll wait, it's OK."

"Don't wait. They're still far off," Mike said persuasively. "Why shouldn't you have as nice an afternoon as I'm having?" He grinned, and slid closer to her. "Lay back."

"No! What if they see?"

"OK, then let's trade positions. You lean against the tree. And close your eyes."

Marcy giggled and swiveled around til she rested against the tree. "I've never done this outdoors before," she whispered.

Mike moved next to her. His hand crept up her wide skirt til his fingers found her center in its white silk panties. His fingers grazed her lightly, sending a hurried shiver through her.

"Lie back," he commanded gently, as Marcy shifted her weight against the tree. She closed her eyes savoring the tingling in her vulva. Unconsciously, she spread her legs wider, so Mike could slide his fingers through the band at her thighs. Marcy squeezed her loins tightly in anticipation. Now Mike rubbed her sensitive spot more urgently til Marcy replied with frantic lurches.

"Oh, oh," she moaned, feeling a wave of heat surge through her. Over and over she arched upward, to no avail. "It's no good," she wailed softly. "I need more. I just can't do it," she panted with mounting frustration. His fingers worked on her, but it seemed pointless, for his fingers just did not provide the friction she desperately needed. Marcy bit her lip and glanced to the fields. The children and their chaperones were out of sight.

"Mike, please," she moaned, pushing his hand against her, urging him to try harder. But it did not work. Marcy groaned, unable to stand the frustrating longing that had welled inside her.

She inched forward til she could reach the fly on his pants. Hastily, she unzipped him, removing his already tumid member from his pants. It bolted upright, as if in waiting. She scrambled on top of him, adroitly slipping her panties off and tucking them in the waist of her skirt so she wouldn't misplace them.

Then, sitting up, she felt his swollen manhood pulsating against her vulva. She jammed against him til the climax shattered them both. They grappled each other, as their wetnesses mingled.

"Ah, finally, thanks," she smiled, kissing his dimpled chin in gratitude.

"Yeah, well, it was tough on me," he grinned. He replaced his member in his pants as Marcy slid off and struggled into her panties.

She breathed deeply, smelling the delicious afternoon, and hoping that the night would sparkle also.

Sometimes she'd hear the tap on her door early, or sometimes late, after her return from Mike's. The Van Couverings didn't begrudge her her social life, because she was always there for them. She was there for them in the bedroom, in the jacuzzi, in capes, and before mirrors, alone, as a duo or triple. Of course this life couldn't last, but it was a blissful game.

Lazily, she watched the two little girls come closer and head for the swing set and ladders. She waved gaily. Alexandra ran up, planted a swift kiss on her cheek and then veered back toward the climbing equipment.

Mike struggled to pull his t-shirt out of his jeans to cover a small stain that had leeched through to his pants. Marcy regarded him frankly. She liked his friendly good looks, his easy charm. He seemed capable and strong, the sort of person she could count on. Like Kurt.

Alexandra and Jessica scrambled onto the glider and by alternatingly leaning forward and backward managed to gain momentum. Giselle and Whit stood off to the side, holding hands, watching. Marcy plucked at a few strands of dry grass next to her, sifting through them. If only she could find a ripe green one, then she'd know spring was really on its way.

Suddenly, Alexandra screamed. Darting up, Marcy saw why.

Jessica had slipped off the glider and was dangling, her foot caught, her head banging onto the rough ground as the glider kept moving. Giselle stood stock-still, unable to move.

Quickly, Marcy raced to the glider, grabbing it to silence it. An enormous gash cut through the entire top of Jessica's head. Blood cascaded out, drenching the girl's face and shoulders. She began crying hysterically as she saw the blood.

"Giselle," Marcy yelled. "Go get bandages. Call an ambulance!"

Giselle didn't move. She stood, her hand clapped over her mouth in horror.

"Giselle!"

But neither Giselle nor Whit nor Mike moved. They could only stare, open-mouthed, at the bloody child cradled in Marcy's lap and the other sobbing one.

Marcy tore her skirt and pressed it to the wound, as she unhooked Jessica's foot and held her head in her arms. Alexandra clung to her neck, beseechingly.

"Go get help!" Marcy ordered. "Mike! Get help."

No one moved.

Unbelieving, Marcy roughly pushed off Alexandra and scooped up Jessica and ran toward the house, calling for help.

"Theresa!" she shrieked as she ran. It seemed to take forever. It seemed as if she ran miles. She heard Alexandra running after her, plaintively calling her name.

At last she seemed to hear Mike's voice, commanding the others to run toward the house too. But she didn't stop, she ran, pushing her skirt hard against the gash to still the bleeding.

"Theresa," she cried. "Help!" The kitchen door opened as the cook stared.

"Oh, Lordy. Come quick, Marcy," she cried out, holding the door for them.

"Quick, call an ambulance!" Marcy cried out, gasping for breath. She mounted the back steps two at a time and ran to the counter near one of the sinks. She sat Jessica down on it.

"Lay her down," Giselle gasped, racing into the kitchen.

"No, don't," Marcy retorted, reaching for paper towels to press against Jessica's head. "Keep it above her heart. Cuts down on the bleeding." She pressed the toweling as hard as she could against the child, meanwhile feeling Alexandra whimpering at her knees. "Oh, Alex, everything will be fine. It's going to be fixed."

"I called," panted Theresa returning from the pantry phone. "They'll be here real quick!"

Marcy nodded, still pressing the wound, trying to stanch the flow. Her skirt, her shirt, her hands were covered in red, as was the little girl.

"Where's the ambulance?" she cried out fearfully. She didn't know if she could hold the blood back. What happened if Jessica died from blood loss? She gingerly raised the towel, eyeing the gash to determine if the oozing blood had slowed down. Why didn't anyone else help her? Why were they all standing there watching?

"Jessica?" she murmured. "I think it's OK." She said it, but she didn't mean it. She just needed to say something to calm herself. But then she looked a bit more thoroughly and heaved a sigh of relief. It was better. The blood had begun to clot. "Oh, thank goodness. It's gonna be fine." She smiled, though a wave of faintness overpowered her, so that she leaned against the kitchen cabinet.

"I think it's better, now." Cautiously, Marcy removed the toweling, and saw, beneath the matted and bloodied hair that the gash was indeed beginning to clot. "I hope it is, Giselle. Do you need to call her parents?"

"Oh, yes, of course," she replied, "yes." Almost hypnotically she headed for the phone.

How could this have happened? Marcy asked herself, replaying the incident. The children were doing the same activity they'd always done safely.

Had they gotten over-tired? Or was it just a freak accident? Had she responded fast enough?

The sound of a siren roused her from her thoughts. Two white-coated women hurried through the back door and went directly to the child, now almost quiet, sucking a lollipop proffered by Theresa. Alexandra hugged Marcy's ankle.

They examined Jessica quickly, saw that while the gash had virtually stopped bleeding, it might nonetheless require surgery. They turned to Marcy for permission to take her to the hospital. Marcy turned to Giselle.

"I—I guess so," she stammered, returning from the phone. "I called her parents. Her mother is coming right over. She will be here in two minutes."

"Giselle, they want to take her to the hospital in the ambulance. What do you think?"

"I—I . . ."

"I think you should wait two minutes," Marcy interrupted. "I think you could scare her in the ambulance. If it's not bleeding, then her mother could take her in the car."

Marcy became aware of Mike and Whit shifting awkwardly in the back corner of the kitchen. Where had they been all this time? Why hadn't they done anything? Why had they all stood and watched the girl dragged on the glider? Why hadn't they offered to help in some way?

Shaking her head to rid herself of these thoughts

163

when she needed to consider the situation before her, Marcy turned to Giselle. "What do you think?"

"Fine. OK," she answered dully, patting Jessica's arm.

Marcy leaned down to pick up Alexandra in her arms. "It's fine, now. Jessica's mom is coming."

The mother burst into the kitchen, and hugged her child. After a few moments consultation, she hurriedly thanked Marcy and then carried her child out to her own car to take her to the hospital. Giselle followed.

One of the paramedics turned to Marcy on the way out. "Good job. You did a good job," was all she said before closing the door.

Marcy heaved a sigh, and found herself trembling. She looked at Mike, troubled. Something about his reaction ate at her.

"I think I better be alone now," she said. "I'll talk to you later."

Mike and Whit nodded and speedily left the house.

How quickly things change, she mused as she pulled her bloodied clothes off and threw them down the laundry chute. Only minutes before we were sitting on the grass in a warm sunny day. And then this. Even with Lord what's-his-name, oh yes, Worthington, the night soured so fast.

But that wasn't the real problem—the changeability of things. It was Mike. He'd done nothing.

What kind of people were Giselle and Whit and

Mike who could not respond to the emergency? They weren't mean, they weren't stupid. Maybe just naïve, maybe they just hadn't seen enough. How strange, Marcy mused. I always think I'm the naïve one, the one who hasn't seen very much.

Suddenly, Marcy knew what was gnawing at her. It was the memory of Kurt, of something that had happened last summer. She remembered when his little brother, Matt, had fallen beneath the lawn tractor. He was nine, and his summer job was mowing the lawn. As he headed up the street hill at too great an angle, the tractor tipped, pinning his leg. Kurt, out back, had heard the tone of the tractor change even before he heard Matt's yelps. He knew the tractor was no longer anchored to the ground. He bolted to the side of the house, to find his little brother pinned. He yelled for Marcy and the two of them heaved the tractor up just enough so that Kurt could pull out Matt's leg.

Quickly, Kurt had removed his shirt to give Matt some warmth even on the summer day, then raced to the house to call the rescue squad. When he ran back, he had the afghan from the living room couch to cover his brother until the medical squad could arrive.

"Ah, Kurt," Marcy smiled fondly at that memory. "Wait'll I tell you about my day." She looked at Alexandra, huddled among the pillows on Marcy's bed, asleep. Silently, Marcy walked to her desk and jotted a fast note to Kurt.

*"I can't wait to see you. As the time gets closer,*

165

*I look more and more forward to showing you where I have lived and introducing you to everyone."*

"So how do I handle Kurt?" Marcy asked aimlessly as she and Giselle lounged on Marcy's great bed. Giselle was polishing her nails scarlet, but Marcy only looked on. Red fingernails were out of the question, and anyway, her nails were too stubby.

Marcy felt comfortable again with Giselle. At first, she thought Giselle would be angry with her for taking over, then she thought she'd be angry with Giselle for doing nothing. But it hadn't happened that way at all. Giselle had apologized. Nothing like that had ever happened before. She'd frozen, terrified. Marcy understood. Maybe if she'd grown up in a city, she too would have frozen.

Mike too had stammered an apology of sorts. Yes, of course he'd seen football and sports injuries. But always there was someone to handle them. And they never bled. They each felt awkward for a few days, and then gradually the old friendships and comforts returned. So now Giselle was propped on Marcy's bed.

"Why don't you tell him everything you've done. That way he'd be able to see the real you," Giselle said, dabbing at the corner of her index finger with a Q-Tip.

"No. I couldn't." Marcy hesitated. "I'm thinking of pretending none of this happened, and just letting him do what he wants with me."

"I don't think you could lie still for it," Giselle answered, standing and stretching.

"I could tell him of one experience."

"What are you afraid of?"

"Um . . . that he may not want me anymore," Marcy said. "It's as plain and simple as that."

"How do you know you'd want someone who held this year against you?"

Marcy frowned in thought. That was a good point. And yet, she hated to disappoint him. He was always so patient with her, so understanding. It was like a slap in the face to say she hadn't ever wanted to be intimate with him, but she'd been happy to be so with strangers. She studied his photo on the bureau.

"There are other things beside sex, Giselle."

"Like what? If you don't have good sex, you don't have anything," she tittered.

"Kindness." The thought of Daniel flashed through her mind. "Inner strength." The thought of Mike standing ineptly, also flashed through.

"But that's not all, Marcy." Giselle stood and peered out the window, stretching her lithe body.

"I know. I want a good time too. But I can't let myself forget the other things that are important to me also." But even as she said this, she wondered if Kurt would have the same physical needs she had. And if he would have the same spirit of adventure. She bit her lip in consternation as she stared at the picture of his wide, grinning face.

167

"Marcy!" Alexandra squealed, pushing open the door. "We're going to London tomorrow. My daddy said he's taking us all for a few weeks!"

"What?" Marcy stared at the girl and then at Giselle in amazement. "When?"

"The day after tomorrow. Or maybe tomorrow. I forget."

Marcy giggled and tousled her hair. "Silly. Are you sure we're going after all?"

"Absolutely." Mr. Van Couvering's voice startled Marcy. "Hello, ladies," he nodded to Giselle and Marcy. "I have a bit of business, and thought it would be a welcome trip."

"Wonderful!" Marcy clapped her hands together. "When? Tomorrow or Friday?"

"Friday. We'll be at the home of some old friends who are, in fact, going to be in New York."

"Ooo, nice," breathed Giselle. *Tres gentil.*

"Well, then, we'd best pack, hadn't we?" Marcy grinned.

# CHAPTER 12

Now Marcy found herself opening closets and peering out the windows of the small bedroom closeted into an eave to see the streets of Knightsbridge below. Knightsbridge. London. It was hard to believe she was here, that she'd been here since late morning, and that aside from a few hours of a nap and a walk through the neighboring streets, she'd not done anything else.

She shivered with excitement. For she awaited Mr. Van Couvering's associate, James Bingham, her escort for dinner. She paced her yellow room with the yellow silk drapes framing two floor to ceiling windows, raring to step forth in her new spring clothes that Mrs. Van Couvering had purchased for her some weeks ago.

Marcy whirled around before the mirror tucked into the closet admiring the navy linen coat dress that just grazed her knees. The large white buttons gleamed beneath the V-neck that just showed the top swelling of her breasts. Rather good, she thought. Vaguely, she wondered if she would have had the judgment to select this dress for herself. But spying her pumps, those steadfast friends, she suspected she wouldn't.

Marcy ran her fingers through her long hair,

169

fluffing it just slightly, looked at the dark circles under her eyes devoid of makeup as well as sleep, and walked down the straight staircase to the front hall.

Like the rest of the house, the front hall was posh and understated with a collection of Hepplewhite chairs nestled against the sides of the large entryway. A long table, filled with lush tulips, graced the center of the room.

The ringing of the bell brought forth a servant from the back somewhere, who then ushered in James Bingham.

Marcy unabashedly stared at the handsome man before her. He was tall, with a full head of black hair and eyes of such blue that to Marcy they appeared almost like the sky at twilight. He had the craggy look of a man whose passion is the outdoors.

James looked at her with frank approval also, at the blonde mane that fell to her shoulders in luxurious folds, and the unadorned, fresh face.

"How do you do?" he asked.

"Very well, thanks." Marcy held out her hand to shake his and immediately felt a shiver as they touched. "Let me get my coat." Quickly, she reached for her light wool black coat laying across the back of the chair.

"I wanted to show you a bit of the city before we meet for dinner," he said in a clipped, elegant voice. He didn't seem immediately warm and friendly as Daniel had been, but rather standoffish and retiring, Marcy thought. But then again, appearances can be deceiving; Lord Worthington was charming.

Marcy slid into the chauffeured Rolls Royce and studied her hands nervously, waiting. Suddenly, this all seemed too grown up, and she felt cast adrift with the strange man.

"I know you've only just arrived, and you're probably frightfully tired, but this little glimpse will acclimate you somewhat. Then, tomorrow you will have had somewhat of an overview."

She nodded. She wasn't the least bit tired. Perhaps she should have been, but it was all too new and exciting. "Take me wherever you think I should go," she murmured.

She noticed that he reddened.

The driver drove along the Thames, past the Tower of London where James recommended she visit the Crown Jewels, past London Bridge, through Trafalgar Square where Marcy eyed the statue of Nelson, around Hyde Park to Buckingham Palace, then down Regent Street past shops that Marcy longed to stroll through.

James chatted amiably, and Marcy found herself drawn to his dry sense of humor, ignoring his slight stuffiness. At last, they joined the Van Couverings for dinner.

"So, Marcy, what do you think?" Mr. Van Couvering inquired as they dined on roast beef and Yorkshire pudding.

"I love it. And my guide is wonderful."

"I would happily fetch you tomorrow for a look at the Tate," James said.

The Tate, the Tate, Marcy speedily wondered to herself. What is the Tate? Why can't I remember? She swallowed, hoping he wouldn't quiz her.

"Gallery," Mr. Van Couvering smiled blandly, noticing Marcy's discomfiture. "A remarkable English and Modern collection."

Marcy winked slyly, to thank him, and turned to James. "I'd love to, but I take care of Alexandra during the day."

"Then in the evening? It is open tomorrow for a special engagement, and I have access. Will you be free?"

Marcy glanced at Mrs. Van Couvering for approval. She nodded.

"Perfect." She smiled into his handsome face. "I plan to go back to my room tonight to read all about the galleries so I won't seem so dumb."

"Ignorant, not dumb," James replied, lifting his red wine glass. "And not unappealing."

Marcy smiled gratefully. For she scarcely knew a thing about London.

"Shall we walk a bit?" James inquired as they left the restaurant. Mr. and Mrs. Van Couvering were off to a private night club to meet some friends, and had left Marcy and James to themselves.

Marcy nodded in assent, although it was after

11:00, and she was finally exhausted. Still, she found him intriguing. She walked silently next to him for a few blocks, til he turned, heading into the dark. He stopped, took her hand and passed it through his arm, as if to protect her.

"Tell me a little about you," Marcy began. "You've told me all about London, not anything else."

"All right." He cleared his throat and pushed his hair backward with his palm. "I grew up outside of London, spent summers in the Swiss Alps with my family, graduated from Oxford, and have been in business ever since. Your employer and I are partners in a venture in Great Britain."

"Are you married?" Marcy blurted.

He stopped abruptly and looked at her. "Why, of course not. Why would I be out with you if I were?"

"Oh," she swallowed, ashamed. "Well, I once knew someone else who didn't quite feel that way. Are you engaged?"

"No. Not at all." He bent down and kissed her briefly on the lips. Marcy responded enthusiastically. She loved the feel of his firm lips on hers.

She felt his strong arms around her as he pulled her closer to him. She wrapped her arms around him and felt the tough, strong back through his suit jacket. Suddenly, she yearned for more.

"Can you come to my flat?" He asked hoarsely, covering her face with tender kisses.

She nodded. Silently, they strode through the

173

park and down unknown streets. It was dark and silent. A bobby passed them and nodded goodnight. Marcy felt as if she were in a netherworld with unfamiliar corners and ghoulish street lamps. But then they were at his building. James led her up the steps.

She stopped in the foyer in wonderment. A huge spiral staircase wound from the marble entrance way up stairs. An immense living room with stately windows faced her.

"Where did you get the beautiful flowers?" she asked, staring at vast vases of lilies and hyacinths and daffodils in the front hall and living room.

"My housekeeper is instructed to take care of that. You see," he slipped off her coat, "I do a great deal of entertaining. I have no regular lady now, so my housekeeper, Mrs. Minnies, attends to these details."

"Did you have a lady?"

"Yes," he murmured into Marcy's ear. "I had a wife. I divorced her some years ago."

"I'm sorry."

"Not at all. It was a mistake for us, and we happily parted. No children, of course." He took Marcy's hand and led her up the staircase. "Come. The library's up the stairs. It's rather a disjointed affair, where I live."

Dutifully, she followed him. But instead of taking her into his bedroom as she supposed he really intended, he took her into a library, just off the top of the staircase. The walls were lined with bookcases and filled with leather-bound volumes. She strained to see the titles.

"Histories," he said, his back to her, as he poured two glasses. "Architectural histories."

"I don't drink, James." Marcy stepped back as he handed her a fluted goblet.

"Not a bit?"

"I'm not 21 yet."

"You don't have to be 21 in this house. It's champagne. To celebrate your arrival."

Gingerly, Marcy put her tongue to it. The sparkles momentarily stung. She put her lips to the glass and hesitantly lifted it. The liquid swilled around within her mouth, a pleasant, though slightly bitter taste, until she swallowed it.

"Mmm," she smiled, and took another sip. And then, not knowing whether the champagne had hit its mark or what she thought was its mark, a giddiness seemed to swell over her. Marcy stepped toward James and lifted her hand to his shoulder. "Thanks."

He raised his shoulder, and turned his head to kiss her hand. Then he put his arms around her and pulled her to him, kissing her hard til she gasped. She placed her hands on his chest to push away for a breath, but instead, found herself hastily unbuttoning his light blue shirt. A navy monogram was discreetly embroidered on the pocket.

A flash of heat swept through her as she fumbled with the buttons. She didn't think she could get to him fast enough. He pressed his thigh

175

between hers, and she felt the wetness spread within her private parts.

James reached down and hiked up her skirt, pushing her panties to the ground. At the same time, Marcy unbuttoned his pants and reached for him. She didn't bother to look at his hard member. She only wanted him to thrust himself inside her. He placed one hand on her breast, kneading her nipple til her entire body throbbed. The other hand played with the wet opening of her crotch til Marcy gasped with delicious anguish. She bent forward and brought his shaft to her. His belt buckle pressed against her stomach. But she didn't care. She only knew she had to have him now. Quickly, overcome with fire, half-clothed, they groped for one another until they found their spots, eagerly pushing together until they climaxed in unison.

The slim champagne glass lay, empty, on its side.

At last, they pulled apart, satiated, smiling at each other.

"Thank you, Marcy. I enjoyed that," James said, promptly righting his clothing. He straightened his tie in front of a small mirror in the hall just outside the library.

"Yes, thanks also." Marcy stopped. "It was rather abrupt, wasn't it?" She missed the langor of long passionate kisses and roaming hands over her body. Somehow tonight she'd felt rather like a machine. She pulled her rumpled skirt down from her waist where he had pushed it in his hurry.

"But, my dear," he replied with surprise, "there's more time. We certainly have many opportunities to explore one another more."

"Ah, yes, you're right," she answered, twisting her skirt so the zipper lined up with her hip. She could see he would be a lusty bedfellow.

# CHAPTER 13

*"Dear Kurt,"* Marcy wrote from the stiff-backed occasional chair in the corner of her room.

She was snuggled in a terrycloth robe that the hosts provided in the bathroom. It had been carefully folded on top of the heated towels. As she stepped out of the shower, she'd noticed a small pipe just under the shelves housing the towels. Gingerly, she reached out for it, to find that it warmed the towels above. Such luxury, she sighed, slipping into the pale yellow robe that matched the color of the room.

In the distance, she heard the double-decker buses roll by. It was easier to feel a part of London than Paris, she thought, tapping the end of her Bic pen against her teeth. She could speak the language, at the very least. But, also, the city seemed more familiar to her than Paris. The buildings reminded her of Philadelphia and her one trip to New York. She almost felt as if she lived here, and yet it was clear she'd been here only a couple days.

Still, she felt as if she'd mastered the Underground and could easily find a taxi. Of course, James had helped in the transition—in more ways than one.

*"Today was fabulous."* Her letter continued. *"Mr. Van Couvering's associate, James, took me to the Tate Galleries and then to the Victoria and Albert Museum. Mrs. Van Couvering suddenly decided to spend the day with Alexandra, so I was free. Tomorrow, he said he'd drive me out to Cambridge where his brother is at school. I'm having a whirlwind of a good time. Last night, since it was our first night here, we had dinner with the Van Couverings."*

No, she thought she'd stop there. She didn't think she should say that she and James had had sex standing in the library with the spilt champagne glass on the rug. Yes, he was abrupt. He lacked Mike's hunger, Daniel's imagination and Mr. Van Couvering's deftness, but he was diligent and competent and, most assuredly, he got the job done.

Even as she thought about his stiff sex pumping against her, she pressed her legs together, trying to stay the tingling that threatened. She'd have a long night of it if she started heating up now.

A tap on her door roused her. "Yes," her voice quavered. Really, she should be dressed. James would call for her in an hour.

"Marcy?" Mr. Van Couvering questioned.

She darted to the door and opened it. He stood before her, fully dressed. He raised a quizzical brow. "An at-home evening?"

"No sir. A lazy *au pair*. Are you going out?"

"Yes. Dinner and theatre. I came to tell you

that Mrs. Van Couvering and I will be off now. Alexandra is with the sitter and asleep." He shut the door behind him. "It is very hard to resist you in that tantalizing state."

Mr. Van Couvering reached out, pulled the sash of her terry robe til it fell open. She stood exposed, her breasts standing before him, the nipples already taut with excitement. He cupped her breasts and bent over to taste their tips.

Marcy glanced down at his pants, and noticed the swelling. Smiling, Mr. Van Couvering nodded imperceptively. She knew what he wanted. She reached out and planted her hand on the front of him. Softly, evenly, she began to massage his manhood til it began to rise further beneath her touch.

"Sir?" she inquired, looking up from under her long lashes.

"I'd say you've become quite accomplished." Mr. Van Couvering stuck his tongue playfully in her ear, then ran it along her neck, to her shoulders and her bosom.

Marcy moaned as he teased her nipples with his tongue and ran his gentle hands along her buttocks. She ran her fingers across his stomach and fumbled for the clasp of his pants. He lifted her and carried her to the double-sized bed. Quickly, he pulled off his pants, as she unbuttoned his shirt and loosened his tie.

Then he lay on his back. His erect member stood upright, ready for action. Happily, Marcy climbed on top of him, laying her body the length of his. Her robe flapped behind her. She wriggled her body against him and felt his moisture against her navel, as he toyed with her breasts. She ran her hands along his shaft til he grunted and gripped her loins tightly with his hands.

Then, swiftly and smoothly, he entered her, filling her cavity with his density. Languidly, they pumped against each other as if there were all the time in the world, stopping and starting with leisurely abandon. She reached down and slipped her finger into his navel, hearing him groan with pleasure. Her other hand played with the hair on his chest. He, in turn, ran his hands over her ribs and firm hips, his finger darting in and out of her anus. Together, with great familiarity, they moved from side to side, as well as up and down, waiting for the embers of hot desire to ignite.

And then they did. Suddenly, Marcy gripped his shoulders, and began to rotate her hips vigorously. He rolled her over, so that now he was on top. She wrapped her legs around his hips as they hammered against each other until they came in a surge of fire.

Marcy felt him touch her hair with his hands and then slide from under her. She watched him, somewhat forlornly, as he quickly dressed, looking as elegant and pressed as when he entered. Although she expected this sort of exit from Mr. Van Couvering, tonight, for some reason, it left her faintly annoyed and forlorn. She hadn't really done all that she'd wanted to do with him. She had wanted even more time with him.

"Have a nice evening, Marcy," he said as she looked after him. He started toward the door, but turned back to kiss her. His tongue filled her mouth and Marcy, despite herself, pressed her hips hard against him. But he pulled back, as business-like and focused as ever.

She smiled. He was easy to be with. Like a worn, comfy shoe. It was always good with him. And she knew his moves so well. But, tonight, she just wasn't satisfied. Really, she would have pre-ferred Mike, of endless energy — or James.

Her eyes glazed over as she thought about the countless times she and Mike could do it. He rarely became flaccid after sex or, suddenly busi-nesslike, bid a hurried farewell as Mr. Van Couvering did. She'd merely rub his shaft between her two palms until it hardened, or she'd take it between her lips until it was ready for her. Or lay on top of him, moving her body rhythmically, rocking against it.

She licked her lips. Certainly, James would be a welcome relief from the lingering incompleteness she now felt. He was most companionable and interesting, not an enormous ball of fire or a giant laugh machine, but steady and kind. He had a nice way of passing on information about the paintings, tapestries and furniture they saw in the museums, or the architectural details of the build-ings they drove by. He acted as if he'd accidently come across the information somehow during the day, when, really, she knew, he had stores of knowledge gleaned from those leather-bound volumes.

"'London, thou art the flower of cities all,'" James had noted that morning as they drove past Regent's Park, admiring the Late Georgian and Regency buildings. "William Dunbar said that. What do you think?"

"I feel like I could live here forever," Marcy replied, nuzzled against the soft leather seats of the Rolls Royce. The interior wood glistened with polish.

"Let's head for the Tate, but first we'll drive past Marble Hill House and Chiswick, to show you the Palladian influence."

Lost in the volley of terms he effortlessly tossed out, Marcy nodded enthusiastically nonetheless, and let herself be led.

James directed her through the Clore Gallery at the Tate to inspect the Turner collection. Marcy sighed with delight as she saw his sketches of the Thames, views of light and Venice, and the watercolors. Entranced, she followed James to see works by Giacometti, Balthus, Rothko, as well as the abstract artists Mondrian and Kandinsky and sculptures by Brancusi.

"Gad, it's so much," Marcy breathed, heading for a bench. "I can't remember it all."

"One must wander through these halls over and over. I daresay the British Museum will also overwhelm you." He sat next to her on the bench.

Marcy passed a sidelong glance at his thighs, their strength clearly visible through his dark suit pants. She hoped he'd want to see her tonight as well. A little less intellectualism would be in order after the lights went down.

"Isn't there anything smaller, that I could handle a bit better?" she asked plaintively. For how could she include all these things in a letter home? She'd have to read from the guidebook her hosts had left in the bedroom to remember everything she'd seen. "What about the Victoria and Albert Museum?"

"I think that would be a top-rate idea, but we'll skip the tapestry and paintings and even the Rodin, and go right for the furniture and silver."

James offered his hand which Marcy gladly accepted to help her stand. Then, contentedly, she placed her arm through his as they strolled from the museum. They lunched speedily and hopped a taxi for the other museum.

"Oh, wow," Marcy gulped as she stared at the Chippendale cabinets, japanned and chinoiserie furniture, the Newdigate and Sprimont silver centre pieces. "What I wouldn't give to have these in my life."

"Many a person has uttered those same sentiments, I'm sure. What do you most like here?"

She shrugged. "I don't know. It's all so beautiful, and I know nothing about any of it. I can hardly evaluate it." She turned, stood on tiptoes and pecked his cheek. "I guess the silver is the most fun for me. Thank you for indulging me, taking me here and there. It's really kind."

He nodded and patted her hand.

Now Marcy stood, folded her letter and slipped it into the envelope, hoping Kurt was less observant than her mother.

Marcy winced in remembrance of her mother's last letter, received only that morning.

*"Be careful that you don't enjoy yourself with too many men. Remember that you are coming home to one man who expects a faithful woman."*

How in the world could her mother tell? Marcy hardly wrote anymore, ever since she sensed her mother's suspicions. Maybe the dearth of letters was clue enough.

The chimes of the clock in the hall outside her bedroom reminded her that her daydreaming time had best be over. James would soon be here. Quickly, she dressed in a black linen suit with a cropped jacket and white silk blouse, and waited for him.

They dined at his private club in the section reserved for men with women, then went to another posh club for dancing. James promised to take her to theater the following evening, but postponed their trip to Cambridge another day because of pressing business.

While Marcy chatted and listened happily, her eye was fastened to her watch. For she coveted his body. Mr. Van Couvering had been the appetizer. She was ready for the main course. Tonight,

James' slightest touch was enough to send spasms of heat through her. In her imagination, she relished the chance to linger over his body, to explore the details of his flesh and have him explore hers. She pressed her thighs together. She wanted him to pluck at her nipples, thrust his hard manhood deeply into her til she cried out. She could barely wait til their departure.

At last, as other couples began to filter out of the club, James turned to her. "It's a bit late, I daresay, but can I invite you to my flat again for a nightcap of sorts?"

"That would be nice," Marcy replied demurely.

She wanted to rip off his clothes here and now, on the very dance floor, as his hand brushed against her breast when he helped her on with her coat. She drew a sharp breath.

As they exited to the brisk spring night, Marcy sighed with relief. Soon. She heard her heels click along the street as they walked toward his home. Where would they do it tonight, she wondered. His bedroom? The library again? Would she have her second sip of champagne in her life? Maybe the dining room table?

She glanced at his long body, the hips that swung easily as he walked slightly ahead to open the door. Marcy could scarcely contain the tingling within her. Calmly, James took her coat and hung it in the closet, then led her into the immense living room. An onyx fireplace commanded center stage. Large beige couches and low, stuffed chairs graced the floor around it.

He pointed to the baby grand piano. "Do you play?"

"No, do you?"

He sat down on the bench, and began to run his fingers over the keys as the music poured out of the instrument. Marcy stood near him, studying the printed name, "Steinway," over the ivory keyboard.

She placed her hands on his shoulders as he moved forward to the music. Then, she touched her fingers to his ear lobes and along the firm face bones. He played on. She glanced down at his pants, but could see nothing save gray pinstripe fabric between his legs.

She shifted, trying to dispel her own heat. He looked up, smiling, his sparkling, even teeth an invitation to her tongue. Marcy sat down on the bench next to him, scarcely able to even hear the music, she was so on fire.

She bent her face around to look at him squarely and planted a kiss on his lips. James lifted one hand and placed it on her shoulder, bringing her around him further. She kissed him harder, and placed a hand on his thigh. She felt it tense under her touch.

"Can you play and do this at the same time?" she murmured, placing her other hand on his manhood. She felt nothing, however.

"Never tried. Shall we?" He returned his hand to the piano. Marcy deftly unzipped his pants.

Surprised, she saw that he was soft. She fondled him through his underwear, waiting for him to harden. After a few moments, she placed her palms on either side, as if to roll the shaft like baking dough under a rolling pin. But it was to no avail.

"Maybe you ought not play," she whispered, sliding to the floor in front of him. His right foot stretched out to the pedal, lifting and dropping to modulate the sounds.

Marcy, never lifting her hand from his crotch, unbuttoned her suit jacket and shirt til her breasts swelled within the tiny white lace bra. She leaned forward, so that the fleshy part fell on either side of his member. She moved back and forth, caressing him with her breasts.

He played on.

"Don't you like Beethoven? *Für Elise?*" James placed a hand on her head, then her neck, but other than that, he played with just his right hand.

"Yes, but sometimes I like this better." Marcy moved back and placed her lips on his tool. What was the matter? she wondered. Why wouldn't he do it? He'd done it last night. She placed her foot beneath herself and wiggled against it, as her own body craved release. Furiously, she ran her mouth, her tongue, her breasts, her fingers over him, but he would not grow hard.

He stopped playing and placed both hands on his thighs, waiting.

"What's the matter?" Marcy looked up anxiously. She needed this, and he was of no help.

He shrugged. "Don't quite know. Occasionally, it occurs." He sat unmoving, smiling impassively.

"Don't you care?" she cried out, consumed with passion.

"Of course. You're very attractive." Now he stood and pulled her to him. He firmly kissed her lips, then placed his hands on her breasts. Marcy pressed against him, willing him to harden, but it would not happen.

"What are we going to do?" she pleaded. She wanted to yank his member til it stiffened. She reached down and wrapped her hand on his scrotom to see if that would help.

"Perhaps in a while. Some champagne perhaps?"

"I don't think so. Unless it will help," she added hopefully, pushing even harder against him, rubbing her entire body against him, trying to come even then.

"It's unclear. You're really excitingly attractive." But his member sat limply.

Marcy reached behind her back and unclasp her bra, freeing her breasts. She smiled at him beguilingly.

James stooped over and kissed them, then placed his hands on them, massaging them almost mechanically. Marcy glanced down at his flaccid member. It sat foolishly outside his pants.

Suddenly, Marcy wanted no more of this

travesty. It was—repulsive. She never thought she'd find any of this repulsive, but here, facing his flabby mechanism, she was utterly repulsed. To see this soft piece of flesh lifelessly hanging before her was almost grotesque.

She shook her head in bewilderment as she broke away from him and began to dress herself again. She'd had seen enough men, felt their admiring eyes and hands upon her to know that she was not lacking. It was he. She'd been a nursemaid for Yves, but she did not intend to be one for a man who could not bring himself to harden.

"Perhaps you could call me a taxi," she simply said. Rapidly, she dressed herself. And she knew she did not want to be with him again. She did not want to spend time punting at Cambridge University or attending theatre. "James, it's not right. I don't think I want to do this again." She turned. "But thank you."

"Right, then, I understand."

Let him return to his volumes on architecture.

Marcy smiled her thanks, but inside felt grubby. No, she didn't feel like a failure, that was clear. Rather, that she'd engaged in something tawdry and unnatural. Men just weren't supposed to be like that, she said to herself as she stood beneath the very hot shower, trying to steam out the evening's loathesomeness.

# CHAPTER 14

Marcy spent the next few days and nights content-edly sightseeing with Alexandra and a hired nanny who showed them appealing sights for children and adults.

"You know," Marcy grinned at Alexandra as they wandered through the zoo in Regent's Park, "that when the zoo opened about 150 years ago, the zoo keepers wore top hats and green coats to care for the animals."

"Didn't they get all yucky?" Alexandra giggled at the thought of the men's spotted attire.

"Probably. Things are a little more down-to-earth now," Marcy responded, taking the child's hand in hers.

She'd had nice days, shopping in Harrod's and darting in and out of the shops on Regent Street. She didn't regret James' absence one bit. In fact, whenever she happened to think of him, she wrin-kled her nose in renewed disgust.

Still, she was somewhat saddened by the absence of physicalness to this trip, for the Van Couverings had been noticeably distant, virtually out all the time. Vaguely, she hoped they weren't angry with her behavior toward James.

"It's time to go to my cousins'," Alexandra beamed, bursting into Marcy's room early the next morning. "You have to meet all seven of them. And you can meet mommy's sister."

Marcy rolled sleepily in her bed. "What time is it?" She turned toward the clock. "Yipes. It's 9:00. How did that happen?" She bolted upright. "You're right. We're getting picked up by them at 9:30."

She threw on some brown linen pants, cropped to the ankle, and a knit sweater, which she'd purchased just yesterday, then quickly dressed Alexandra in some cordoroy overalls and shirt. She gathered the clothes they'd need for their few nights and raced down stairs to the sunny blue and white breakfast room for hot cereal and scones. No time for tea now, she thought grimly.

The car would be here in ten minutes. They'd drive out alone, for Mr. and Mrs. Van Couvering had gone to Beaseley Park yesterday afternoon.

The driver drove them north, past St. Albans, Ascott House and Woburn, past little stone homes and thatched roofs and, later, vast manors. "It looks like *Northanger Abbey*," said Marcy softly to no one in particular.

"Who's that?" Alexandra quizzed, scrambling to her knees to see better.

"A book by a lady called Jane Austen who lived a long time ago. She wrote about a young woman my age who visited a huge estate like that. Then she got married and lived happily ever after."

Marcy smiled. That would be a nice life, to marry into one of those families, but so far the English men she'd met weren't exactly what she'd want to spend a night with, much less the rest of the nights in her life.

Glumly, she wondered what these few nights in a country manor would have in store for her. All she knew was that Mrs. Van Couvering's much older sister had married someone when young, had some children with him before he died, and remarried just a few years ago and had some more.

As they drove up the tree-lined drive toward the manor house, Marcy's eyes bulged at its beauty. Formal gardens dotted the landscape. Stone statues and benches lined the paths to the fields, surrounding woods and the ballustrade framing the swimming pool. The house itself was fit for royalty, surely 80 rooms, though Mrs. Van Couvering's sister, Julia Swain, later noted that a large portion of the manor was closed off.

"Not many of my sons are here any longer. Just the girls, really," she said. Her voice was neither quite British, nor quite American. "More?" Mrs. Swain nodded toward the teapot.

"No, thank you. I've had quite enough tea," Marcy smiled. She'd miss elevensies, that morning tea and pastry, when they left England. She'd have to start the tradition herself in Delaware. Even as she thought that, she knew there was scarcely a month left there. Soon, she'd leave all this. And return to what had become the unknown.

But now she smiled at Mrs. Van Couvering's sister who, though slightly taller, otherwise was identical: hair, mannerisms, makeup, facial structure. But, unlike Mrs. Van Couvering, she was outgoing and outspoken.

"Will William take you in the carriage this afternoon?" asked Mrs. Swain as they sat about the tea table in the morning room overlooking a rose garden, just beginning to show signs of new life.

Marcy smiled. She'd met the tall, strapping William as she arrived. He was just returning from fishing. He looked like Kurt, with high rubber boots over his thighs, a tam, and several rods. They'd smiled frankly at one another.

"He said he'd take me in the cart," Marcy replied.

"Watch that he takes you in the carriage and not the cart. Or you'll be in for a bumpy time of it."

"Oh, mum."

Marcy wheeled around at his deep voice. He had just entered the room, still dressed as he'd been in the morning. She smiled in greeting.

"Mum, she's a farm girl, she told me."

"Then she'd most certainly want to ride in something she's not accustomed to."

"We'll test her mettle."

"See if she's made of metal, I daresay," Mrs. Swain retorted jovially.

Marcy's head spun from mother to son. What a

194

jolly family. Just like mine, she thought wistfully, suddenly missing her sisters and parents.

"I'll take whatever you want me to take," Marcy offered.

"That's the spirit. The cart's hooked up to Big Bill outside the kitchen." William bowed gallantly. "Sorry, mum. Maybe one of your other sons will take a young lady in the carriage."

Marcy giggled. For Julia Swain had several to choose from. She had three of her own sons from a first marriage, two from her husband's first marriage, and two little girls from their marriage together. Happily, Mrs. Swain waved goodbye and Marcy and William clambered onto the cart.

They rode silently, and Marcy knew they needn't speak. It was almost like being with Kurt. They seemed to know each other. They instinctively knew that each liked the outdoors and the smell of hay and spring flowers and heather on the fields.

"This is beautiful," Marcy said. "Thanks for taking me out. What's that?" She pointed to a small stone house at the edge of a drive.

"My cottage. That's where I live. Not in the big house. This stuff, it's not for me. I want to work the land, be closer to it. I manage the farm and work with the hands."

As the cart bounced along, he explained that he intended to modernize the hundreds of acres his family owned and maintain the land that had been in his family for hundreds of years. Marcy

195

nodded, at once understanding what he meant. That was why Kurt would not leave High Flats. Certainly, the land hadn't been in his family for generations, but it was theirs anyway.

When they came to a dirt road, William pulled over and climbed out, offering his hand to Marcy. But she jumped out unaided. Impulsively, she looked at him, just her height, and kissed his cheek.

"I'm sorry," she mumbled. "Rude of me. But I'm just so happy here. It feels so great."

"Quite all right with me." William took her hand, guiding her over a stream and through some brambles til they settled on a grassy knoll overlooking the farms.

"You know, I feel like we've known each other for ages. Maybe it's just being with another outdoor person. I dunno." Marcy shrugged.

She liked his craggy looks. He wasn't handsome. His reddish hair with unevenly cut, a front tooth was broken, light freckles dotted his face, his finger nails were dirty, his clothes were stained. And yet he was good humored and kind, and as she whiled away the afternoon, interesting. He'd graduated from London University two years ago, and had returned to the farm, much to his mother's horror. She'd wanted her sons to be businessmen, not farmers.

Lazily, Marcy slipped off her shoes, feeling the spring day. She dug her toes into the grass and recalled another day like this—it seemed eons ago—when she and Mike had fiddled around. Glancing at William, she saw him watching her. She smiled gently.

He leaned over and kissed her lips softly, running his tongue around the inside of her mouth. She shivered and opened her mouth for a further invitation. He thrust it in, completely filling her.

Softly, he lay her back on the grass and ran his strong hand on her calves and over her thighs, firmly pressing and rolling them under his strong hand. Marcy quivered with joy and opened her legs. He moved his hand to her inner thigh and then to her mound. He grunted as he kneaded his fingers against the soft flesh. She groaned and turned toward him, hoping to press herself against him.

Marcy reached out and placed her arms around him, bringing him closer. Swiftly, she lifted his torn shirt from his pants and ran her fingers around his navel. He grunted and lurched against her. They ground against one another through their clothes, yearning for more, yet careful not to proceed too quickly.

In the distance, Marcy heard birds singing and water gurgling, signaling the beginning of spring in England.

William rolled her onto her stomach, and then lifted her to her knees. He edged behind her. He pulled her blouse out of her pants and slid his fingers up til he found her breasts. Quickly, to help him, she unbuttoned her blouse and slid it off.

From behind, he grasped her breasts, massaging them and running his fingers around their tips til they were hard with pleasure. Silently, she unfastened her pants and wiggled out of them. She reached behind her and felt for his manhood, now pulsating beneath his pants. Expertly, she unzipped him and felt him pull off his clothes.

She turned her head slightly to enjoy the sight of his firm rod about to enter her. His hands separated her thighs further and then, adroitly, he slid into her. She gasped with joy at the first touch and pressed back feeling his body against her buttocks.

Marcy dug her fingers into the coarse grass of the knoll as he lunged into her over and over and pressed her nipples. Then suddenly, as she felt that giant spasm welling within her, he withdrew, settling back on his haunches.

"Why are you stopping?" she panicked. "Don't."

"But I must," he grinned. Then he took her and guided her back on to the grass.

She lay, her legs wide open. "Now, do it now," she urged, unable to bear the craving.

He leaned over her and placed his mouth on her breast. She squirmed, trying to shift her body beneath his, but he skirted her efforts. With his other hand, he toyed with her soft mound. She reached for him, trying to drag him by his rod to her.

Then, finally, after when seemed hours of

delicious torture, he mounted her, setting his strong, stalwart body on top of hers as he inserted himself into her cavity. They pumped in unison until great waves of ecstacy cascaded over them both. Marcy lay back, panting with exhaustion and happy release.

"At last," she sighed contentedly.

"At last what?"

But she only shook her head. This was not the time or the man to tell about her Lord or the piano-playing James. At least there was one man in England for her.

"Well, then," he lay back against the grass, his head propped on his arm. "Don't tell. Everyone should have a secret."

Marcy snuggled next to him, laying her head on his bare chest. Soon, though, she felt the coarse rye grass pricking against her skin. "I think my butt's being gouged to death," she giggled, standing. "And, anyway, I think I should get back to Alexandra."

"Quite right." William stood also. They dressed quickly and returned.

A few stones against her window that night roused her from lethargy. She'd been staring aimlessly into the fire, not thinking of much beside her return to London in two days and to the Philadelphia Airport the following day. This trip had ended up wonderfully, she sighed. She'd seen London and the English countryside and met a variety of men.

Now she peered down into the courtyard at William's grinning face. There was something so boyish about him. Imagine throwing stones at a window. She waved. He beckoned. She shook her head, for, really, where would they go? And what if she got caught? It seemed so unseemly to run out with Mrs. Swain's son. Mr. and Mrs. Van Couvering were just down the hall.

William beckoned again, but she shook her head, and turned away. A few moments later, she heard a tap from the corridor, and the door opened, unbidden.

He stood before her with his impish grin and clean clothes. She faced him in her flannel nightie and bare feet.

"I came to say goodnight, m'lady," he grinned, bowing, as if he hadn't spent the past few minutes throwing stones at her window.

"I feel like I'm in the 18th century when I'm here," Marcy backed toward the warming fire. The nights were still cold.

"Precisely why I'll not be part of this life." He walked over and placed his hands on her buttocks. "What a fetching little wench you are," he said softly, his lips grazing her cheek, eyes, and ears.

"Oh, I don't think this is right," Marcy murmured, backing up. But the fireplace was behind her.

"Of course it is." William's hands began to press and squeeze her nipples. She didn't move, hoping to discourage him. "You're not hurting anyone.

200

And in two days it will be a fond memory."

She looked at him startled. He was so plain-spoken about the end of the relationship. Do it, have fun, no strings attached, and never again. But she had entered no liaisons that way. She expected more than one night stands. Yet, of all the men she'd met, he was the most like her. He took the least stretching of the imagination to envision a future with. But he was quite plain that he intended no future with her. Just a couple nights.

And, surprisingly, that was fine with Marcy. She glanced at him as he toyed with her nipples with sensitive, agile fingers.

The familiar tingling began to spread through her body as she eyed the man before her with his lopsided grin and shaggy hair. She glanced down at her breasts, surprised they carried so much power. She wiggled toward William, trying to line up her mound with him.

"Shh, I will show you something you didn't know. Lean back, lean against that wall and relax."

Marcy obeyed and closed her eyes as he fiddled with her nipples with his fingers and his lips and tongue. And then suddenly, bewilderingly, the giant spasm of orgasm overcame her. She reached out and gripped his shoulders til she was spent.

"I didn't know that could happen," she gasped. She grasped her breast in her hand, awed at its sensitivity.

"Now, let's get down to business." Swiftly, William pulled her nightgown over her head, and peeled off his own clothes. Gently, he bent her over on all fours before the hearth, and then mounted her from behind. "I like this way," he murmured as his body covered hers from above. "The animals do it this way. They must know something."

Marcy reached back for his scrotum which she gently played with in her cupped hand, as he touched all parts of her body. Her arm rubbed against his inner thigh and she felt him tense to her touch. He reached around for her feet and explored her soles and toes with a deft touch. Then he moved around to touch her vulva. He pushed against her more rapidly, as he fingered her with care and expertise. Faster they pumped against each other til they came in a flood of passion, grunting and groaning with release.

Flushed with delight, they bid each other goodnight, knowing that tomorrow night would be their last together.

# CHAPTER 15

The first thing Marcy did when she was alone in her room in the Delaware mansion was rip open the letter from Kurt. She'd safely put her trip to England away, and had come back contentedly to the United States.

But now, her heart stopped in fear. For he'd at last told her the day and time of his arrival in Philadelphia. It was finally happening. The dreaded event.

Not that she didn't want to see him in the abstract. But this letter signaled the end of a magnificent year of introductions: new people, new sights, new—how could she put it delicately—experiences. Soon she would return to old acquaintances, familiar sights, and the absence of the physical pleasures that she'd come to know.

But more importantly, she must decide. What should she say to him? Did she ever want to see him again? Did she want to marry him, as planned? If she did, what would she say to him? Pretend she was the same sexual *ingenue* she was when she left? Pretend she was just a little less so? Tell him everything? She grimaced at this thought.

Then, let's say she determined what she would say to Kurt, what, in fact, did she want from him? The novice she'd left? A sexual rake? What happened if he couldn't perform up to her expectations? Were her expectations too great for any one man?

Marcy paced the floor in thought. For he would be arriving in three weeks, to spend a final week here, in the east, before returning to High Flats with her. Her heart thumped. Should she call it off for six months and stay on til she could make up her mind? She bit her lip til it bled.

Giselle would say, "Don't go back. Have fun still. You're young." Sigrid would say that also. What about Mr. Van Couvering? She'd never ventured to ask his opinion about anything. She'd counted on him always to take care of her physical needs, but would he have insight into her emotional ones as well?

Perhaps she should see Kurt and then make up her mind. If it wasn't right, she'd pay for his air flight. That seemed like a feasible idea. At the very least, it put off the final decision.

Marcy undressed slowly, carefully hanging her clothes back in her closet. If she waited til the morning, the maid would do it, but she needed something to do now. She heard Mr. and Mrs. Van Couvering's laughter on the staircase and peeped out of her room.

Their arms were around each other and she nuzzled against his chest. With a pang, Marcy realized she wanted to nuzzle against someone's chest also. Funny, she thought, as she watched them stop on the mid-level landing and kiss one another, she no longer considered casual lovers appropriate.

"Ah, Marcy," Mr. Van Couvering caught sight of her.

Gulping, Marcy opened her door, as if she'd intended to go somewhere. "I'm sorry, I was going to get some milk. Then I saw you and didn't want to disturb you."

"No disturbance. Why don't you tell her, my dear?" He looked fondly at his wife.

"We're going to have a baby," she said softly. "Another baby."

"Oh, that's wonderful, just wonderful!" Marcy clapped her hands together. But, in fact, she did not feel so gleeful. A sudden emptiness pervaded her. Then a sense of loss. Everything as she had known was changing. Even if she stayed on, it would now be different. And when she left, even her memories would not be the same. For the family would change as it grew. She would fast be replaced by the new baby and the new *au pair*.

She swallowed. What a long day this was turning out to be.

Trembling, Marcy stood at Gate 4 waiting for Kurt's flight to arrive. She'd been here two hours earlier than necessary. The chauffeur remained in the car reading a newspaper.

She clenched her fists together in trepidation, and felt perspiration begin to spot her forehead. For, although she had decided what to divulge to Kurt, she did not know if the opportunity would arise. Nor did she know precisely what she would say. But she did know that she would do nothing to terrify him.

Fearfully, she started as the announcer called Flight 210's arrival. She wiped her wet palms on the side of her beige linen pants and shifted her shoulders, trying to relieve the unexpected discomfort of her great old cotton bra that she'd put on that morning.

She scanned the sky, looking for a low flying plane, then turned toward the gate, nervously. Even now, even as she had determined that she would not say anything to appall him, she wasn't sure she really wanted him. She was no surer, after three weeks of almost constant thought, of what she really wanted. Her eyes clouded over once again in consternation.

"Oh," she gasped, her heart skipping a beat. For there, not four feet in front of her, was her stolid, rock-hard Kurt, his blonde hair closely cropped, his square face smiling. He dropped his soft bag before her and held out his arms.

She went to him, and buried her face in his neck. "Oh, Kurt, I am so glad to see you." And she was. The fears melted as she felt his strong arms crush her to him. She lifted her mouth to his and pressed her lips hard against his lips, then opened them slightly as his tongue probed the edge of her mouth.

He broke away, and held her back. "Marce, Marce," he muttered, calling her by the name only he called her. "You're lookin' real good, real good."

She looked at him, happily. How could she even think of telling him all that she had seen and done this year? How could she hurt him?

"Come on, the car's waiting," she chirped, taking his hand. He lifted his bag with the other.

They chatted easily the entire ride back to the mansion. She pointed out the vast estates, the Chateau Country it was called, promising to return to Philadelphia to visit the waterfront area, the capitol and the wonderful zoo. He told her about his family, about their friends' marriages and break-ups, about his work on the farm, about her mother and father, and sisters. He didn't say much about himself.

"Say, Marce," Kurt lifted her hand and held it on his lap. "I missed you. I missed you real bad."

She nodded, an unexplicable knot building in her throat. Suddenly, all the things she planned to say—and not say—fell aside.

"Me too," she mumbled. And while she definitely did not want to hurt him, she didn't think she could not tell him about her year. How could she start a relationship with such massive deceit?

They spent the afternoon in the gardens with

Alexandra and her friend Jessica and Giselle. They dined with Mr. and Mrs. Van Couvering, who extolled her virtues. Then, nodding goodbye as they went out for the evening, Marcy showed Kurt his room in the guest quarters, next to the room Lord Worthington had occupied.

She looked at him, unpacking his bag, with his hard, strong back bent over his belongings. Marcy longed to take him in her arms, feel the power within him. But she did not know how; only this Marcy could do it. Not the Marcy she had been, not the Marcy he'd known.

Instead, she stood hesitatingly, at the door, her hand propped on the brass door knob.

"Nice room, isn't it?" she swallowed.

"Yeah." Kurt emptied the travel bag and placed it in the closet.

"Big, too. Much bigger than my room at home."

"Marce," Kurt stood straight, facing her, a length away. "I don't want to talk about rooms."

"You don't like architecture?" she said brightly, nervously twisting her blue skirt with one hand while the other clutched the door knob.

"I want to talk about us," he said brusquely.

"Ok," she answered smiling gaily. "What about?"

"I came here to see you again, to see if you and I still had something going between us."

"Yes?" she asked tentatively. "What do you think?"

"So far, I like what I see. What about you?" He sat at the edge of the dark, brocade-covered bed.

"Oh," she breathed with relief. "Oh, me too. I was so afraid, Kurt. You can't imagine. I thought maybe I changed too much," Marcy babbled uncontrollably. "You know I've seen a lot since we've been away from each other. I thought you might not like that. And then I thought maybe you had found someone else in High Flats or near there." She paused for a breath, but cut him short as he opened his mouth to speak.

"I know that you saw Mindy Allen a few times because you told me that. But then you stopped writing about her, so I thought maybe it had become serious, and you wanted to tell me that in person. I've met a lot of people too, been to a lot of places." A warning voice cautioned her, and she stopped again, and released her twisted skirt and the door knob.

She clasped her fingers together before her. "Of course you could have met zillions of new girls, or found old girls were interesting. You didn't talk much about the girls you were with. But I know you were, because my sister Sally saw you with this blonde girl who sort of looked like me." Marcy glanced at him.

"Whoa!" he held up his hand. "Hold on. All those things happened. I went out with a lot of girls. I thought, 'This is when I'm supposed to see if Marcy is for me, and if I want to settle down now.'" He stopped abruptly.

Anxiously, Marcy looked at him. She took a step forward. "Did you? Did you?" She wanted to say more, but her tongue throttled her words.

"I didn't find anyone I liked better, if that's what you mean," Kurt smiled reassuringly, and patted the space next to him for her to sit down.

No, that was not what she meant. "That—that wasn't exactly what I meant."

"You mean, did I do it?"

She nodded shyly.

"Yup," he replied softly, looking down. "It didn't come to anything," he added quickly.

"Did you do it a lot?" she asked, curious, as she sat next to him.

"A little," he answered evasively.

But she knew there was more, and he was embarrassed.

She nodded, and waited for him to ask her so she could deceive him, but he said nothing. Instead, he turned and put his massive arms around her, drawing her close to him. He put his lips to hers, and with this tongue, entered her mouth, searchingly. She replied, opening wide, shivering as his hands roamed over her back and hips.

He lay her back against the brocaded pillow sham and kissed her hard, his tongue filling her mouth deeply, his hands running over her legs and shoulders and hips. But he would not touch her breasts. She ached with longing. How could she tell him to touch her?

Fearfully, she reached for a roving hand and placed it on her breast. He cupped it in his with a sharp intake of breath, and murmured her name over and over. "I love you, Marce, I love you."

She clung to him, tears of relief filling her eyes, for that is what she had missed. Someone telling her he loved her. She strained toward him, hoping to slip her body underneath his, but he stayed to one side, the bulk of his size resting against the bed.

Kurt placed his hands on her cheeks, framing her face. Tenderly, he kissed her eyes, the tip of her nose, her ears. His breath came faster. His hand, laying lightly on her breast, began to delve more deeply, pressing the flesh til she turned toward him, desiring the feel of his body.

"No, I don't think so." Kurt broke away from her and rolled to his side.

He shook his head and sat up. She glanced down and saw an enormous rise in his pants. She wanted nothing more than to reach down and caress him til they moaned with joy together. Instead, she simply rolled to her side, and propped herself on her elbow. Her hair fell into her face. How would she convince him? Should she convince him and spill the beans she was trying to handle so carefully?

Marcy lay still, pondering. Would they spend the night this way, side by side, as if they were children in High Flats at the lake? She stretched out her hand, lifted his and placed in on her hip.

She leaned toward him and kissed him lightly on his lips.

Suddenly, almost urgently, he came toward her and rolled her to her back, even as he slid on top of her. His body covered hers. She felt his stiffness through his clothes but did nothing more than wait. She would wait for him and be, again, the virgin she once was.

Slowly, moaning with love and lust, Kurt fumbled with the buttons of her starched white cotton shirt. One after the other, deliberately unfastened. He hiked himself up to look at her breasts, tightly gathered in the white schoolmarm's brassiere. With the tips of his fingers he began concentric circles round and round til he landed on the ends. His hands dropped beneath her back to unhook the bra clasp.

The bra slid loose from her body.

"Ohh," his mouth lunged for her nipples, suckling at them and grinding his hard body onto hers. She answered slightly, trembling at the feel of his tongue on her flesh.

"Oh, Marce, I don't want to stop," he whispered into her ear, his breath flooding her body with untold passion. "I have thought about this night over and over." He buried his face between her breasts, kissing and caressing them tenderly.

"I love you, I love you," she said softly. "Please."

"I want you." He groped for the zipper of her pants. She felt him push the sides apart. She kissed his forehead, running her fingers over his back, feeling his beefy muscles through his shirt.

He sat up, breathing hard to stare at her, once more in her high-waisted underpants. Gruffly, he pulled off her pants and her shirt and brassiere. She lay before him in just her panties. She didn't dare touch him, though his prick, stiff and rock-hard within his pants, cried out for release. All she needed to do was reach out and unzip him. But she just stared, scarcely able to bear the tension welling within.

"Oh, God, Marce, you're beautiful." His hands slipped down under the waist of her panties and explored her tuft, then dropped lower to her moist privates. She spread her legs for him.

Then he lifted her hand and placed it on his belt. "Do it," he said invitingly.

Marcy needed no second invitation. She unhooked the belt, and pulled the snap on his jeans. She stopped and returned her arms to his back where she gracefully massaged him.

She sucked in her breath, trying to silence her quivering.

"Marce, do it," he said hoarsely, as his fingers toyed with her cavity.

Wriggling from the heat of his touch, Marcy unzipped his pants and spied his erect member pulsating within his underwear. She moaned with desire, desperately wanting to clutch it in her hands, thrust it into her mouth, shove it into her body.

"Well?" he asked. "Will you?" he repeated politely.

Marcy nodded, staring in wonder and delight at the massive member before her. Gingerly, she touched it, gently rubbing the shaft with her fingers til it seemed, somehow, to stiffen even further.

Awkwardly, Kurt pulled off his pants and shirt and then slid on top of her, his manhood pressing against her navel. They pressed against each other with only their underwear separating them. His hands feverishly roved over her body, fondling every crevice, even as she touched him.

But still, he would not go beneath their underwear. They ground against each other, but the material forbade his entrance. She strained against him, willing him to enter her. He grunted. "I want you," he moaned, kissing her breasts and belly hungrily. "Will you take me?"

He moved down so that his tip just touched her entrance, moistening her even further. She writhed in answer to his question.

"Take me," she moaned, flooded with unquenchable tension. "Oh, do it," she clung to his back, pushing him closer.

Instead, he moved down on her and with his face pressed against her underwear, he toyed with her mons through the cotton.

She cradled his head in her hands, pressing it further against her. In this unspoken way, she hoped to tell him that she desperately craved more.

Then, almost tentatively, with one finger, he stretched the elastic waist band and peered down at her private parts. She heard him groan, saw his eyes roll upward in ecstacy. Slowly, he pulled them down to her upper thigh, then further to mid-thigh, then her knees. Marcy wriggled out of them.

Kurt snuggled up to her pussy and put his tongue to her. He touched her gently as she wriggled at the sheer joy of his touch. She entwined her fingers in his hair as his tongue lapped at her til she groaned in unfettered desire.

He lifted his face and smiled his friendly smile. She returned it, waiting for him. She longed to go down on him also, so together they could make their music. But she would not.

Kurt slid upward again, lazily kissing her taut stomach and the curves beneath her breasts, her shoulders, neck and face. Marcy closed her eyes, waiting. She thought she would explode. When would he do it? When would he take that hard rod out of his pants and shove it into her? Fiercely, she gripped him, urging him to enter her at last.

His hands roamed her body, relentlessly sliding in and out of the folds of her behind and pussy til she lurched back and forth in unceasing frustration. She moaned, inwardly pleading for him to enter. Then, thankfully, she felt him wriggle out of his underwear and felt him lay against her again. For the first time she actually felt his turgid manhood pressed against her body.

She wanted to see him, admire the firm flesh, but more than anything, she wanted him inside her. She pushed her hands against his butt, pressing him against her. And then he slid his throbbing penis within her. She groaned as he filled her cavity. They grunted as they felt each other. Marcy wrapped her legs around his waist as tightly as she could, and followed his rhythmic movements as he pumped his body against hers.

He heaved against her harder and faster. She pressed back, the two grinding furiously against each other, as she clawed his back and opened her mouth to his thrusting tongue.

She screamed out as the heat began to suffuse her limbs. It overtook her in a wild frenzy of blinding colors and mesmerizing senses. He lunged against her, and wild white heat hurtled through them, showering bits of fire into every pore.

They pumped against each other some more, until the embers of fires had been stomped out. He fell against her, his body as wracked with the sweet smell of sweat and exhaustion as hers.

Marcy laughed with delight. He could match anyone! She flung her arms around his neck and kissed his cheek vigorously.

"Whoa, ma'am, that was some tussle," he grinned, rolling off her. Lazily, his fingers roamed over the curves and folds of her body. Marcy lay against him, wrapped in a delicious haze.

After a few minutes, Kurt sprang from the bed.

"Race you to the shower."

As the water pelted them, he took her again, standing. She leaned back against the white tiles, chest heaving. Then as Marcy toweled him dry, her now-expert fingers lingered on his shaft, til he stiffened again. This time he took her on the carpeted floor to another shattering climax.

And finally, they had headed toward the bed. She eyed his soft member and sensuously licked her lips as she watched Kurt's gaze on her naked loins. Even as she lay back among the pillows, she saw him harden to thick, long proportions. She leaned forward, wondering if she dare take him by mouth? Would he suspect anything of her past if she did?

Saying nothing, she grasped his manhood between her lips, flicking her tongue over the tip and running it along the rod, until his hot fluid spurted into her mouth.

Yes, Marcy thought with pleasure, he was good, he was strong, he could last forever.

Now, they lay next to one another, her head cradled in his arm, her fingers toying with the blonde hairs on his chest, her leg thrown over his.

"Marcy, how many times have you done it?"

She stiffened. The interrogation was not supposed to go this way. He wasn't supposed to know. "What do you mean?"

"You're no virgin." Kurt leaned on his arm, forcing Marcy off his chest.

"How about you?" she retorted, stalling for

time. Terror spun a web through her. How could he tell?

"Asked you first." He didn't move. "Who have you done it with? How many times?"

"I—" She stopped. Sweat festered on her forehead.

"Who?" He pressed, his voice harsh.

What was she to do? Tell him about the nights with the Van Couverings? Yves? Daniel? Mike? Lord Worthington? James? William? Even as their names and faces flashed through her mind, she trembled with the fear that he could read her thoughts. Would she say he was mistaken, that there'd be no one? Or would she say there'd been just Mike? Or Daniel in France?

"I—" she started and stopped. Should it be with someone he could see, like Mr. Van Couvering or Mike, or an indistinct European?

"Who?" Now, Kurt sat up completely. "I'm not going to be taken as a fool." He stood and reached for his clothes.

Marcy glanced at the clock. 1:15. Surely, she should just bid him goodnight now and think about it in the morning.

"A man in France," she retorted, her eyes filling with tears.

"Is that it?"

She closed her eyes with shame. Ashamed that she was lying to him, ashamed that she hadn't the courage to meet him head on with the facts of the heady, giddy wonderful things she'd really done.

218

Marcy shook her head, no.

"Who else, when, what else?"

And Marcy told him. She blurted out the names of everyone, one after the other, like the roll call from a town meeting.

When she was done, she looked at him, pleadingly. Silently she begged him to accept her once more. She held out her arms to him.

"Get out of here. Just get out."

"Please, Kurt," she whispered plaintively.

"Get out, just get out." He turned away from her and strode toward the window.

"Kurt, please," she pleaded. "You don't understand."

"I understand, all right." He stretched his arms forward so that his palms rested on the window before him. He bowed his head forward.

"No, no you don't," Marcy said. "Please, don't leave me. What can I say to make you stay with me? What can I say to erase this conversation?"

"Marcy, get out. Get out," he repeated harshly. He shook his bowed head from side to side.

"No, I can't." She came toward him and grabbed his shirt tail.

Angrily, he shook her hand off.

"No," she wailed, "don't let this happen. Please don't. I'm sorry. I'm sorry. Don't let this happen." She sobbed. She reached out for him, tentatively touching his shoulder with her fingers. Again, he brusquely shook her off.

"Get out of here," he said through gritted teeth.

He turned toward her, eyes blazing with anger and sorrow. "Get the hell out of here."

Horrified, Marcy backed out of the room.

# CHAPTER 16

Mechanically, Marcy returned to her room, stifling her sobs til she could throw herself against the vast pillows on her bed. How did it all end so suddenly? The bliss that turned to horror? Even as her body was wracked with sobs, she thought that so many of her relationships had ended that way. They'd gone from utterly wonderful glory to unadultered horror.

It didn't matter with Lord Worthington or with James. It had mattered with Daniel. But, now in retrospect, even that relationship palled. No one, absolutely no one, could hold a candle to Kurt. She hurled herself against a pillow and grabbed another to her body, clinging to it for an anchor to sanity.

What should she do? Clearly, she was ruined in High Flats. She could never see her family again, for Kurt would return and tell everyone why. Perhaps she should ask the Van Couverings, after all, if she could stay on, even though she knew they had engaged another young girl for next year.

She clenched the end of the pillow between her teeth. It had been so right with Kurt. They did fit together so well: their goals, their backgrounds, their habits, their bodily needs. And now? He'd hardly said a thing to her, but the bitterness of his voice, the harshness of his eyes had said more than enough.

She knew, without him telling her, that he would return home tomorrow. She also knew that she could not keep him here, that there was nothing that could convince him that she was worthy of him. How could she let him go? She had to find some way to keep him here at least another day.

And if he went, what would happen to her? She'd never been on her own before, cut adrift from a boyfriend. Even as she met different men during this year, she'd always known, in the back of her mind at least, that there was someone for her. She wasn't totally alone in this world. But now she was.

She would find someone, somehow, somewhere to love and be loved by. Perhaps it would be Mike after all. Or someone else at the University. Or another friend of Mr. Van Couvering's. No, it had to be Kurt. Seeing him again had convinced her, more than she could have thought possible, that they was meant to be together.

"Oh, please, please," she moaned, hugging the pillow to her. "I don't think I can stand this." An enormous well of pain grew within her. She rocked back and forth, trying to calm herself. But it was to no avail.

Marcy sobbed herself to sleep in the final hours of the night.

"Good morning," she said stiffly at the breakfast table in the morning. Alexandra was opposite her, as usual, Kurt next to her. "Shall I find out about flights?" She swallowed.

"Where are you going?" Alexandra piped up. "I thought you were staying for a few weeks."

"I have some business to do that I didn't know about," Kurt answered kindly, staring at Marcy til she blushed.

"Oh, like my daddy. He's away a lot, too." Alexandra returned to her cereal.

Marcy glanced quickly at Kurt, but he had fastened his eyes to his plate. She stood. "Almost done, Alexandra?" she asked brightly, for she was to walk the little girl to her friend Jamie's for a few hours. That would give her the time she needed to talk—somehow—to Kurt.

Hurriedly, she escorted Alexandra, nodded hello to Jamie's mother, and returned home. She didn't know what she would say to him. She would beg him to give her a second chance, to try her again. Even as she said that, she knew it was silly. You don't get a second chance at being a virgin.

She careened up the stairs as soon as she returned home, heading immediately for Kurt's room. The door was open.

"Kurt?" she called hopefully, stepping inside. But her heart stopped. For his bed had been stripped by the maid. She dashed to the closet. Empty. His bag was gone. He was gone.

Madly, she ran down the back staircase to Theresa in the kitchen, the perpetual purveyor of information. "Is he here?" Marcy breathed, pushing open the door. "Where did he go? When?"

Theresa looked at her, her large brown eyes sympathetic. "Lawrence took him not five minutes ago. You have a fight?"

"Where?" Marcy screeched, desperate to find him.

"Logan. The airport."

"Oh, God," Marcy moaned. "How will I get there?" Her fingers flew to her throat, as if she were suffocating. "What can I do?" She paced the floor. Giselle. That's it! For as generous as the Van Couverings had been to Marcy, she'd never had access to a car as Giselle had. That was her only chance. If only Giselle were there and could help her! She dialed her number, her fingers shaking.

"Faster," Marcy said between her teeth. "Drive faster, Giselle."

"No, absolutely not. Jessica is in the back seat. You do it my way or not at all," Giselle retorted sharply.

"I'll miss the plane. I've got to stop him at the gate."

"I will not get killed for romance."

Marcy nodded mutely. She gripped the edge of the seat as another wave of panic washed through her. Giselle drove so slowly and Lawrence drove so fast. What happens if the plane leaves before I get there, she asked herself. What'll I do? Don't let him leave, she prayed silently.

As soon as the car slowed before the terminal, Marcy jumped out, calling her thanks. She bolted inside the building, scanning the large area for the stocky, stalwart body she knew and loved so well. He was nowhere to be found. She bit her lip, panic slowly rising.

She glanced up at the television monitor listing the flights and departure times. What number would he be? Ah, there were the destinations. Nothing, she found nothing remotely close to High Flats. Gone, he'd gone, she screeched inwardly. No, look again, calmly, she told herself. Get a grip.

She scanned the monitor once again. Ah there, she breathed. Flight 218, not leaving for 25 minutes. Gate 4. The same gate at which Kurt had arrived yesterday. Was it only yesterday? Relieved that he hadn't yet departed, Marcy felt as if her problems were solved, scarcely realizing she had not begun to confront them.

She raced down the corridor toward Gate 4, her pumps clapping against the linoleum floors. And there, just ahead, about to pay for a newspaper, she saw him.

"Kurt!" she screamed. "Kurt, please!" She ran toward him, tears falling down her cheeks. "Please."

He glanced at her, then turned away, toward the gate.

Marcy grabbed his navy windbreaker. Roughly, he pulled away, forcing her to drop it.

"Please, you must listen." She jumped in front of him, forcing him to stop. He stopped, still gripping his bag, ready to move at the first opportunity.

"We have to talk," she sobbed. "You can't just leave. I have to explain."

"We have nothing to talk about."

"Yes, yes we do. At the very least, I have to apologize, and tell you why," she blurted. She clasped her hands before her, as if in supplication.

"Explain what? *Why* you screwed everyone in sight?" he asked sarcastically.

"Why it happened. How it happened. I didn't do it blindly. I had relationships with them, they weren't strangers."

"Does that mean, whenever you meet someone, you'll screw him if you think he's interesting?"

"No, no," she shook her head from side to side. "I was alone. I was experimenting, trying things out this year." She stopped. "Can we talk?"

"We're talking."

"I mean privately." She glanced around. Several people were looking at them from their seats in the lounge.

He looked at his watch. "I have 20 minutes."

She nodded, acquiescing, and headed to a corner for two orange plastic chairs anchored to each other by a silver metal bar.

They sat side by side. Marcy clenched her hands

226

on her lap. "What are you angry at?"

"I'm not angry."

"Hurt by?"

He stared straight ahead. "You said you wanted to talk. I'm listening."

Marcy bit her lip for the great effort. "I—I want to apologize." She gulped. What if he wouldn't accept the apology? Then what would she do?

"For what?" He said bitterly. "For screwing everyone? Well, that's not good enough."

Marcy heaved a sigh. What did he *want?* Clearly, she'd have to explain something. A mere apology wasn't enough. What she needed to do, of course, was erase everything. But she couldn't.

Slowly it dawned on her. She might not be able to win him back. Maybe he was so thoroughly repulsed that he could hardly bear to see her.

She spread out her hands in exasperation. "I don't know if you're hurt because I broke a promise to you. But if *I* did, then so did *you.* And then, neither of us is worthy of anyone else."

She laced her fingers together tightly. "I don't know if you're hurt because, after all our time together, you were not the first one. But I wasn't the first one for you either. So we're even on that score, also.

"Or I don't know if you're hurt because there wasn't just one person, but several. But *you* didn't have just one person either." Marcy sighed with resignation. She didn't know what else to say, what else she could use to convince him that she hadn't been so terribly bad, that he hadn't been so terribly wronged, that whatever she had done, he had done also.

"You told me that the girls who you were with meant nothing to you. My—experiences meant nothing much to me. They were people to be with and try out. Just like the girls were for you."

He turned to her, his blue eyes blazing. "It's different for a guy."

"Why?" Marcy flashed.

"We have needs." He smacked the fist of one hand into the palm of the other.

"So do we." She glared at him. She was silent for a few minutes. "You know," she said slowly, a hideous thought crossing her mind, "there may be no point in this. Maybe we're too different after all. Maybe, even if we got married, there'd be too great a gulf between us.

"Maybe once I agreed with you, that girls could sit home and guys could go out and drink and have girlfriends, and it was OK, because girls were different. But that was before I knew anything. That was before I met and talked to people. But I don't feel that way anymore. Maybe—maybe we are too different this way to ever work out." She stood, sorrow weighing on her.

"Kurt, I loved you. I guess I still do. But you're beating me up for something you did too. If it's OK for you, then it's OK for me." She shrugged, not knowing what else to say to him.

She felt a giant weight lifted from inside. She

had told him the truth. She hadn't kept anything from him, and she had told him exactly what she felt. For the first time, in fact, she had determined how she herself felt. At least, now, if he accepted her, there would be no deceit.

She looked down at him, tears welling. She sat on the front edge of the chair. "I don't hate you for what you've done with those girls. I just accept it. I say to myself, 'That was the past when I wasn't there. But when we marry we make a commitment physically and emotionally.'" She swallowed, noting the glazed look in Kurt's eyes.

He nodded, and stood. He glanced at his watch. "I have five minutes." He leaned down to grab his bag. "If I don't make this plane, I have to wait five hours." Still bending, he stopped talking. Then he added, "I guess we should talk some more."

Marcy heaved a sigh of relief. "OK," she mustered, slight hope rising within. She sat back heavily on the plastic chair. Kurt joined her. Hesitantly, he reached for her fingers and laced his through them.

"It's not so easy to get used to what you just said. It's a different way of thinking."

Marcy nodded again, still silent.

"I don't mean that exactly," he spoke slowly in concentration. "I always told people that girls and guys should do the same things, that they should be treated equally. I guess when I said that, I meant they should be equal in their jobs. I don't

think I ever thought about sex when I said that."
He heaved a sigh.

"I guess it should be totally true but it's one
thing to say something, and it's another to really
believe it when you're faced with the fact." He
looked down, his finger scraping at some mark in
the plastic. "I don't know what to say now. I
understand what you said to me. I don't feel good
about it."

"Do you think I'm dirty or something?"

"Just like a used car. Like they cleaned up the
seats and the rugs and the dash. They vacuumed
out the motor. But it's still got 75,000 miles on it."
He glanced at his watch. "Missed my flight, I
guess."

"You're right. I've got some mileage. But unlike
a car, I'm just revving up," she giggled, then
clapped her hand over her mouth, embarrassed at
her reaction in this serious situation. "I'm not
gonna wear out. And the thing is, I'm not old and
worn out. I don't have any diseases. I don't need
replaced parts," she carried the metaphor further.

"But you aren't new."

"You're right. I'm not." There was nothing
more she could say to that claim.

He was silent for a few minutes. Marcy sat
quietly also, knowing that these were critically
decisive moments. He was thinking now. He was
finally weighing all the evidence and making up
his mind.

He looked up and swiveled around to look at

her. "OK, Marce." He spoke thoughtfully, as if, even in these last two seconds, he was making up his mind. "Let's try again."

"Oh, Kurt," Marcy threw her arms around his shoulders, suddenly weak. "I'm so glad." Sudden sobs of relief and joy wracked her body. She leaned against him, til they ebbed to nothing. He put his arms around her.

"How'll we get back, Marce?" He grinned that lopsided grin of his.

"Lawrence will come back. Giselle was going to stop by and ask him to come get me," Marcy smiled timidly, still too exhausted to believe he had accepted her back again.

Kurt helped her stand. "Lemme trade in my ticket, girl, and then we'll go find him."

Laughing, they linked arms and headed for the ticket booth.

"Lawrence," Marcy leaned toward the partition between the front and back of the car. "If Mr. Van Couvering ever looks at the dashboard, he's going to wonder how the car put on all this mileage in one morning." Marcy laughed giddily, confidently placing her hand in Kurt's.

"Miss, he told me to make myself available to you," the chauffeur replied.

Maybe he had an inkling something like this would happen, mused Marcy, as she let her fingers drift around Kurt's palm. He closed his fingers tightly and pulled her closer. Swiftly, he planted a kiss on her neck.

"Have any more free time today?" he whispered, his tongue flicking her ear.

Marcy felt herself moisten rapidly. "I'll make some, you can count on that." She nestled against him, and saw Lawrence discreetly roll up the one-way mirrored glass between them. Languidly, she let the fingers of her other hand drift over Kurt's strong thigh.

His muscles tightened. The hand, carelessly draped around her shoulder, dropped forward to rest on her breast, and tenderly massaged it. Teasingly, Marcy lifted her hand and placed it on Kurt's chin. She traced his profile with her forefinger. She leaned over and gently nuzzled his ear lobe and blew into his ear.

Kurt's fingers drifted to her nipples, and traced smaller and smaller circles around it, til Marcy thought she would burst. She longed to have him take her right then and there. She glanced down and saw the bulge pushing against the blue jeans. Kurt saw her glance, smiled and teasingly squeezed her nipples, til Marcy writhed with delicious agony.

"Let's wait," she breathed, her breath coming quickly. "Let's make it perfect." With a great force of will, she primly removed her hand and his hand and sat up straight. "So," she smiled brightly, "what do you think the weather will be like the rest of the day?"

Scarcely able to contain her excitement, Marcy

dashed inside and phoned Alexandra at her friend's. Did she want Marcy to fetch her now, or did she want to stay on? Did she want to spend the day, or just an hour or so? Should Marcy bring over her bathing suit, or would she borrow Jamie's? On and on, she questioned her, insuring herself that she was not neglecting her final duties to the little girl.

In the distant eight-car garage, she saw Mr. and Mrs. Van Couvering head out in her red Mercedes. Gone for the day. Ever since the announcement, they'd been together more and more. Once a pang had passed through Marcy, but no more.

Eagerly, she turned to Kurt who waited patiently at the kitchen door talking to Theresa. "Come, let's go for a walk," she said. She winked at him.

She strode ahead, her hips swinging in the full skirt. Underneath, were her black lace panties and black demi-bra. She'd never looked so forward to any experience before. Now she longed for the perfect ambiance, with the soft winds of spring above them, and legions of time for subtle caresses.

They headed down the stone paths toward the woods. As they reached the edge, the paths changed from white stones to well-worn pine needles, meandering through the trees. They walked on and on, arms about each other, without speaking, knowing only that they were searching for the proper spot to consummate their new commitment to one another.

"The gazebo," Marcy gasped. "Come." Ahead, perched on an incline was the wooden gazebo, an invitation to them. No pine needles would prick their backsides, no sticks would dig into their thighs, no poison ivy would crawl up their spines.

As soon as they had both stepped inside, they stopped and faced each other, wide smiles creasing their radiant faces. Kurt drew Marcy toward him. "I love you, I always have, I always will," he mumbled, kissing her lips, eyes, cheeks and neck.

Marcy drew her breath in sharply. She didn't think she could wait. She was wet with craving. "Take me," she murmured. "Take me now, and then again and again." She fumbled at his shirt buttons and his jeans' fastenings so she could grab him tightly to her. She lifted his hard sex from his pants and bent down, placing a delicate kiss on its tip.

She looked up from under her long lashes as her tongue toyed with his swollen member. He moaned as she rolled her palm along the shaft, feeling it stiffen still further. As she caressed him, he undressed her, carelessly dropping her clothes to the floor. He stopped at her little lace bra. "I like this, Marcy," he breathed, kissing the fleshy swell above the lace cups.

Marcy broke away from him and strutted to the far side of the gazebo. Beguilingly, she sat on the seat so he could admire the firm stomach, the lean thighs, and the scanty lace coverings. She lifted her legs and bent her knees alluringly.

"Ah, girl, I can't stand it."

"Come and git me, then," she giggled, flipping her blonde hair over her shoulders.

Kurt stepped forward and bent to his knees. He ran his hands over her body with soft, firm movements. She shivered. Then, he reached behind her and unfastened her bra. Her breasts draped down over her chest.

"Ahh," he breathed, mouthing her nipple. With his other hand, he dropped her lacy panties to the seat. "You are some sexy number," he heaved.

"I hope it is always so," she whispered back, burying her fingers in his short hair and kissing his neck. She slid off the seat, to her knees on the floor. They faced one another.

Then he stood so he could kick off his clothes. Marcy took his scrotum in her cupped hands and lapped at the large penis upright before her. Expertly, she ran her tongue over him. He rammed himself so deeply that she thought she'd gag, but she didn't pull back. She pressed her finger to his anus. He moaned and withdrew. He lay down, his back against the wooden floor, and settled Marcy atop of him. He guided himself into her cavity, then gently, pushing her backward between his legs, as he lay between hers. Clasping hands, with slow, delicate wriggling, they enticed each other, til they verged on a climax.

Kurt moved first, disconnecting them. He placed her on top of him, so she lay the length of his body. A paroxysm of desire overcame her as he touched her vulva with the tip of his tool. She groaned and moved down on him, inserting him as deeply as he would go.

Panting, he rammed into her, crushing her beneath his weight. She gripped him still harder, as she climaxed over and over til the last throes of passion were spent.

Now, she lay her head on his chest, glistening with sweat.

"Marce, Marce," Kurt murmured. "This is gonna be great for us." He extricated himself. She sighed as she felt their dampness mingle together.

"Do you still want five kids?" she murmured, sliding off him. She stretched, her firm loins tightening. "And that big white farmhouse on Blackberry Hill that we always liked? And one of the Murphys' litter?"

"Yeah," he rolled to his side, his eyes appraising her. "Do we have to go back?"

"Mmm, probably." Marcy stepped out of the gazebo and walked, naked on the pine needles. They pricked her bare soles, but she relished the slight sensation. It merely heightened her happiness. She breathed deeply, stretched her long arms above her, lifted her generous breasts upward, pulled her lanky legs to their full height. Her stomach stretched tightly across her hips.

"How about now?" Kurt whispered huskily from behind her. He pressed her to him, so that his hardening cock lay between her buttocks. He reached around and cupped her breasts in his powerful hands. He moved them tenderly, as he kissed her neck and shoulders.

Marcy reached behind, and ran her fingers over his stomach. He drew his breath in sharply. Then she found him poised and waiting. Swiftly, she spun around, and hopped upward. He caught her as she wrapped her legs around him. She moved slightly so that he could enter her. Together, they moved in the forest, their private parts wet with desire, their bodies moist with heat.

"Ohh," she cried out, pushed frantically against him. He held her tighter, as their bodies careened against each other til the crazy passion overcame them again.

She clung to him, resting her head on top of his, half dazed with fatigue and longing. Reluctantly, she pulled away and slid to the ground. "Nice, Kurt. But I think we have to go. I still have a job to do here. Five days for Alexandra. Five nights for you." Her blue eyes gleamed.

"I hope I can wait for the night," he smirked. He reached for her hand and they headed for the gazebo and their clothes.

Hand in hand they wandered back toward the house. Marcy saw Mr. and Mrs. Van Couvering heading up the drive in the Mercedes. She waved blissfully. For she no longer had the pang of envy, nor the regrets at leaving that she'd once had. For she had her own glorious future.

# CREMORNE GARDENS

### ANONYMOUS

**An erotic romp from the
libidinous age of the Victorians**

## UPSTAIRS, DOWNSTAIRS . . .
## IN MY LADY'S CHAMBER

Cast into confusion by the wholesale defection of their
domestic staff, the nubile daughters of Sir Paul Arkley are
forced to throw themselves on the mercy of the handsome
young gardener Bob Goggin. And Bob, in turn, is only
too happy to throw himself on the luscious and oh-so-
grateful form of the delicious Penny.

Meanwhile, in the Mayfair mansion of Count Gewirtz of
Galicia, the former Arkley employees prepare a feast
intended to further the Count's erotic education of the
voluptuous singer Vażelina Volpe – and destined to
degenerate into the kind of wild and secret orgy for which
the denizens of Cremorne Gardens are justly famous . . .

*Here are forbidden extracts drawn from the notorious
chronicles of the Cremorne – a society of hedonists and
debauchees, united in their common aim to glorify the
pleasures of the flesh!*